ALMS IN THE NAME OF
A BLIND HORSE

Gurdial Singh was one of the most important Punjabi novelists of his time who was also internationally honoured by the Punjabi-speaking diaspora. The National Book Trust has translated his *Marhi Da Diva* in all Indian languages and the Sahitya Akademi has similarly honoured his *Adh Chanani Raat*. He has also been translated into Russian and other foreign languages.

Rana Nayar is a translator of poetry and short fiction from Punjabi to English. He has more than forty volumes of poetry and translation works to his credit. He is also a theatre artist and has participated in a number of major full-length productions.

ALMS IN THE NAME OF
A BLIND HORSE

A Novel in Punjabi

GURDIAL SINGH

Translated from Punjabi by
RANA NAYAR

RUPA

Published by
Rupa Publications India Pvt. Ltd 2016
7/16, Ansari Road, Daryaganj
New Delhi 110002

Sales Centres:

Allahabad Bengaluru Chennai
Hyderabad Jaipur Kathmandu
Kolkata Mumbai

ISBN: 978-81-291-3731-9

First impression 2016

10 9 8 7 6 5 4 3 2 1

The moral right of the author has been asserted.

Dedicated to
The struggling, voiceless millions in our land
Who are yet to find their voice

Introduction

Gurdial Singh: Life and Times

As I sit down to reflect on the range and quality of Gurdial Singh's fiction, Plato's famous dictum inevitably comes to my mind. In his *Republic*, Plato is believed to have stated that he looked upon a carpenter as a far better, a far more superior artist than the poet or the painter. For Plato, the carpenter embodied the image of a complete artist, or rather that of a total man. After all, wasn't he the one who imbued the formless with a sense of structure and form and infused the rugged material reality with untold creative possibilities?

By all counts, Gurdial Singh answers the Platonic description of a complete artist rather well. Born to a carpenter father, who insisted that his young son, too, should step into his shoes, Gurdial Singh chose to become instead, a carpenter of words, a sculptor of human forms and a painter of life in all its myriad hues. On being refused funding by his parents for education beyond the matric level, he decided to be his own mentor, slowly toiling his way up from a JBT teacher to a school lecturer, from there to a college lecturer and finally, a professor at the Regional Centre of Punjabi University at Bathinda. As one of the most illustrious exponents of Punjabi language and culture, he has served its cause for well over six decades now.

Though he started his literary career by writing a short story, Gurdial Singh first tasted success as a novelist when he published his first major path-breaking work, *Marhi Da Deeva*, in 1964. Translated into English as *The Last Flicker* (Sahitya Akademi, 1991), it was hailed as a modern classic soon after it appeared in print. However, his early success didn't stand in the way of, or turn into a disincentive for, his later, equally powerful and significant works of long fiction, such as *Unhoye* (1966), *Kuwela* (1968), *Addh Chanini Raat* (1972), *Anhe Ghore Da Daan* (1976), *Parsa* (1991), among others.

Despite his immense success and popularity as a pioneering novelist in Punjabi, he continued to nurture his first love for short fiction. Indeed, he has authored as many as ten collections of short stories so far, the more notable among them being *Saggi Phul* (1962), *Kutta Te Aadmi* (1972), *Begana Pindh* (1976), *Rukhe Misse Bande* (1982) and *Kareer Di Dhingri* (1991). In addition to *Marhi Da Deeva*, three other novels of his viz., *Addh Chanini Raat* (*Night of the Half-Moon*, Macmillan, 1996), *Parsa* (NBT, 2000) and *Unhoye* (*The Survivors*, Katha, 2005), are also available in English translations.

Tall and gangly, Gurdial Singh is modest to a fault, and has consistently shunned media attention and unnecessary publicity. Recognition has certainly come his way in the form of countless awards and honours, national as well as international. Among others, special mention may be made of the Punjab Sahitya Akademi Award (1979), the National Sahitya Akademi Award (1976), the Soviet Land Nehru Award (1986), the Bhai

Veer Singh Fiction Award (1992), and the prestigious Jnanpith (1999), the highest literary honour in India. Having retired from active teaching and research, he now writes and lives in Jaito, his home-town.

The Tradition of Punjabi Literature

Much in the manner of other world languages, Punjabi literature, too, had its early beginnings in poetry. A Sufi strain was very much in evidence in the compositions of Baba Farid, a twelfth-century saint, often seen as one of the early practitioners of Punjabi poetry. For almost three hundred years thereon, until the advent of Guru Nanak Devji on the scene, Punjab went through an extended, nightmarish phase of foreign invasions, bringing its literary/cultural march to a sudden, temporary halt. However, once the Guru's bani had begun to resonate through the fields of Punjab, soaking into and fertilizing its large tracts, there was no looking back. Some of this philosophical and mystical bani ultimately found its rightful place in the Guru Granth Sahab, a true repository of the collective wisdom of the Sikh gurus and other proponents of the Bhakti movement. In Punjabi literature, the Guru Granth Sahab occupies the same pre-eminent, canonical position that is often conceded to the Bible in the realm of English literature.

The Beginnings of the Punjabi Novel

The novel, however, did not emerge in the Punjabi language until the latter half of the nineteenth century, initially developing largely in the shadows of its European counterpart. Bhai Vir Singh, one of its early practitioners, who was known primarily for his historical romances, sought inspiration in the fictional works of Walter Scott and his ilk. Under the reformist influence of the Singh Sabha Movement, his successor Nanak Singh sought to break away from the imitative efforts, rooting the novel in the very soil and substance of Punjab. Turning to indigenous modes of storytelling such as quissas, popular in the medieval period, Nanak Singh gave to the Punjabi novel a distinct local character and habitation as it managed to reclaim its vital link with the oral tradition.

Ideological Inheritance of Gurdial Singh

Until the times of Gurdial Singh, two diametrically opposed ideologies, viz., a brand of naive romanticism and an indigenous form of realism, had continued to exert pressures and counter-pressures upon the content and/or form of the Punjabi novel. Apart from these ideological tensions, which helped shape the aesthetic concerns as well as their articulation, Punjabi fiction had continued to shift back and forth between the rural and the urban, the past and the present, the poetic and the realistic. The historical importance of Gurdial Singh's fiction lies in the fact that it sought to encapsulate the dialectics of tradition and modernity, even tried to attain a rare synthesis of the two wherever possible, something that had eluded Punjabi fiction until then. Conscious of his role in reconstituting the novelistic discourse, Gurdial Singh ruptured the tradition of the Punjabi novel from within while continuing to nurture it from without.

Gurdial Singh could very well be seen as an exponent of the regional novel, in the sense in which Thomas Hardy and R.K. Narayan essentially were. In novel after novel, he has assiduously recreated a fictional replica of an insulated, enclosed, provincial world of the Malwa region, where he has lived all his life and whose dreams and desires, folklore and culture he best understands and empathizes with. However, the self-limiting nature of the Malwa region does not in any way prevent Gurdial Singh from giving an artistically wholesome expression to the complexities of life he has set out to explore.

Gurdial Singh and the Radicalization of the Punjabi Novel

Gurdial Singh radicalized the Punjabi novel or re-inscribed its ideological and/or aesthetic space by infusing into it a new consciousness about the underprivileged and the oppressed. Commenting upon his first-ever novel *Marhi Da Deeva*, published in 1964, Namwar Singh, an eminent Hindi critic, is believed to have said: 'When the novel was a dying art-form in Europe in the middle of the nineteenth century, it was Tolstoy's *War and Peace* that resurrected faith in novel as a form. In a similar fashion, when in Indian languages novel was going through its worst ever crisis, Gurdial Singh's *Marhi Da Deeva* revitalized this form as only he could.'

The significance of *Marhi Da Deeva* lies in the fact that for the first time ever in the history of Punjabi fiction, a social and economic outcast, leaping out of his shadowy terrain, made it to the centre stage of fiction-scape. While seeking to project the sufferings and agonies of the hopelessly marginalized individuals as well as social classes and castes in a rather involved manner, Gurdial Singh has never lost sight of the imaginative and creative demands of his own vocation as a novelist. Steeped in history without being explicitly historical, his fiction mediates its way through myriad, often disparate, crosscurrents of the mainstream and folk traditions of storytelling, latent in both orature and ecriture.

Gurdial Singh's Fiction: An Overview

In one of his novels, *Parsa*, a low-caste siri, Tindi, requests his benevolent master to tell him an 'interesting' story. On being asked as to what really makes for such a story, Tindi first hesitates and then shoots off a counter question: 'Why are the stories always about kings and princes?' More than a mere rhetorical question, it is the very raison d'être of Gurdial Singh's counter-narratives. He is no less than a messiah of the marginalized, who has consistently and tirelessly tried to put the dispossessed, the dislocated and the de-privileged at the centre of his fiction. From a poor, illiterate farmhand, a small-time worker or peasant to an overburdened rickshaw puller or a low-caste carpenter, it is always the primal rawness of human life that strikes a sympathetic chord in him.

Conceived as victims of social/historical tyranny, most of his characters fight back even in the face of an imminent defeat. He strongly believes that man's ultimate dharma is to fight the tyranny and oppression built into his situation. This is what often imbues his characters, even his novels, with a definite sense of tragic inevitability. This tragic sense is more pronounced in his early novels, such as *Marhi Da Deeva* (1964) and *Kuwela* (1968) than it is in his later works. While Jagseer in *Marhi Da Deeva* is an easy prey to the machinations of a beguiling feudal power play, Heera Dei in *Kuwela* stands firm, refusing to cringe before a taboo-ridden society.

However, the heroic or revolutionary potential of his characters began to come fully into play with the creation of

Bishna in *Unhoye* (1966) and Moddan in *Addh Chanini Raat* (1972). Unlike Jagseer, both Bishna and Moddan not only steadfastly refuse to become accomplices in the process of their own marginalization, but also make untiring efforts to rise in revolt. They even go so far as to interrogate the dehumanizing social and legal practices working against them, but stop short of overturning them. It is their lack of self-awareness that ultimately makes failed revolutionaries out of them.

With Parsa, a Jat-Brahmin, moving centre stage, the dialectics turns inwards. *Parsa* (1991) has widely been acclaimed as an important cultural text, a triumph of Gurdial Singh's lifelong commitment to the art of fiction. In *Aahan* (2008), Gurdial Singh has explored the ways in which the Praja Mandal movement and Jaito morcha, two significant political developments in the history of Punjab, dovetail into the national freedom struggle. Against this backdrop, he has portrayed a very sensitive and sombre picture of a village, Karamgarh, and its hapless people, who first face a natural calamity in the form of a swarm of locusts, and then are subjected to economic and political oppression by the establishment.

There's both a touch of authenticity and self-absorption about Gurdial Singh's ability to fashion a wide range of human characters. For him, man is essentially a social and historical being. As a natural corollary, his characters remain intermediate agents, individualized yet typical concretizations of the context in which they live and operate. He believes that a character is not only important in himself, but also as a vehicle of an idea or an ideology. Both the personal and the collective aspects of character/characterization are equally important for Gurdial Singh, and his portrayals often maintain a delicate balance of the two.

Gurdial Singh's creative imagination is imbued with a rare sense of synthesizing power. Like a true artist, he understands the dilemmas and conflicts of both art and life exceedingly well. He is a minimalist in the true sense of the word, as he manages to make it not just an expression of his style, but also the very texture of his vision and thought. No wonder, he is able to strike a precarious, though fine balance between the narrative and the dramatic, the personal and the historical, the political and the artistic.

Anhe Ghore Da Daan: A Perspective

Anhe Ghore Da Daan is a significant cultural text, a sort of contemporary classic. It derives its title from an ancient myth associated with the churning of the ocean, in which Lord Vishnu was less than fair in his dispensation of the nectar to the Asuras, supposedly the progenitors of latter-day Dalits. Through this novel, Gurdial Singh emphasizes that just as the Asuras had to depend upon the arbitrary dispensation of the Lord, in the same way, the modern Dalits, too, have to depend on the mercy and compassion of the village overlords. On the days of lunar and solar eclipses, Dalits still ask for alms in the name of the blind horse (which in the myth is shown to pull the chariot of Rahu and Ketu, who despite being Asuras, had partaken of the nectar through subterfuge, while it was being distributed only among the Devtas).

The events of the novella are confined to one such day of lunar eclipse in the lives of its characters. Often, it is believed that poor, landless and marginalized characters such as Melu, his bapu, his chacha Partapa etc., lead banal and uneventful lives, which are not even worthy of description, let alone artistic treatment. Exploding this myth, Gurdial Singh has created this 'whirlpool of a novella' around a spate of events that enmesh the hapless lives of his characters, all in the course of a day. The story begins in the early hours of dawn, when Melu's bapu is rudely jolted by the unexpected news that Dharma and his family, who belong to the same caste as he, have been uprooted from the house they had lived in for more than twenty years.

The paternalistic feudal order that had supported their existence and provided for their sustenance is now threatened with collapse, as the market value of land has shot up considerably, slowly giving way to the surreptitious entry of capitalism into the village economy. Now the owners of the land are of the view that it makes much better economic sense to dispossess Dharma and his family and sell the land to factory owners. When persuasion doesn't work, coercive and ruthless methods are used in collusion with the police and the panchayat. Even the collective strength of the Dalits fails to make a dent in a world insulated by an uninhibited display of power, money and influence. The choices before marginalized characters like Dharma, Melu, and several others like them, are limited: either go down fighting against a tyrannical system, or migrate to a nearby town in search of alternative modes of livelihood. Even the town offers no easy palliatives, as is revealed through the (mis)fortunes of Melu and his friends who struggle to survive in one such town, apparently against all odds.

Displaced from the village and abandoned by their own community (which nurtures false notions of how they are living in clover in town), they struggle hopelessly to find a resting place there. Lost to both the worlds, these characters ponder over their never-ending dilemmas and conflicts as they oscillate back and forth between the two extremes of 'home' and 'homelessness'. Not only does Gurdial Singh present a very authentic and poignant picture of Dalits in a Punjabi village, caught in the throes of change and flux, with its rigidities of caste politics and prejudices still intact, he also gives a clarion call for social and political change by asking them to make a clean break from crippling traditions and customs.

Towards the end of the story, the Dalit panch reprimands one such seeker of alms, saying, 'Nothing will change till you stop colluding in your own oppression.' The novella ends on a positive note of consciousness-raising.

Anhe Ghore Da Daan: Approaching the Novella

Let me now talk about the specific features of *Anhe Ghore Da Daan*, so that we are able to understand how this particular novella is different from Gurdial Singh's other novels. Unlike other novels, in which he covers one particular phase in the history of Punjab, *Anhe Ghore Da Daan* is not set in a particular historical period. Notionally, it is set in the times of transition, when the paternalistic model of rural, agrarian economy in Punjab was being threatened with collapse and technology was slowly entering into urban life. By this reckoning, it would perhaps relate easily to the 1960s, the pre-Green Revolution period, when the dialectics of tradition and modernity had just about begun to operate in Indian as well as Punjabi society.

Apart from this, Gurdial Singh has made no conscious effort to locate the novella in a particular time frame. Incidentally, in this novella, he has not created a big story of a small man (as he is known to have done in some of his other novels), but he has created a small story of several small men, thrown together in similar situations by fate and circumstance. In other words, he has sought to create several micro-narratives within the frame of a single macro-narrative. As such, it was but natural for him to have paid special attention to the temporal scheme of the novel, which is confined to a single day. The total 'narrative time' of this novella is around twelve hours, as the story runs through a complete diurnal cycle, from dawn to dusk. The novella begins in the early hours of the morning and ends somewhere before midnight.

On the radar of the novella are, of course, 'little earthquakes' in the life of Melu, a Dalit, and his family—all that could possibly happen in the course of a single day to turn their lives upside down. The main narrative is, however, simply a pretext for focusing on several other Dalit lives, shuttling hopelessly between the two worlds, rural and urban. Gurdial Singh appears to be suggesting that while there may be nothing momentous or monumental in the lives of his Dalit characters, their daily struggle to stay alive and survive against all odds is so compellingly heroic that it deserves our attention as well as sympathy. For him, the diurnal sameness and mundane routine of their inconspicuous lives is only a thin veneer, beneath which he recognizes a seething cauldron of raw emotions, energy and passion, waiting to explode on to the surface.

Unlike most of his novels, which are usually divided into smaller segments or chapters (with the exception of *Parsa*, of course), this is a seamless narrative, not by accident, but the result of a carefully crafted design. By refusing to divide it into chapters or sections, Gurdial Singh has not only created an extended 'narrative about oppression' (that portrays the unrelieved agony and unmitigated suffering of his characters), but also a 'narrative of oppression', one that communicates this sense of unrelieved tedium and oppression equally forcefully to its unsuspecting readers. As we read the novella, we are slowly drawn into the world of the multiple forms of oppression afflicting the daily lives of these characters. With the help of this narrative strategy, Gurdial Singh not only brings alive the oppression of his characters, but also communicates the same to his readers, with a gnawing sense of inwardness.

Moreover, it is in this particular novella that Gurdial Singh has managed to strike a balance between 'silence' and 'language'. Most of his characters do not necessarily speak (in fact, the major characters, including Melu, his bapu, his *bebe*, his sister and brother speak only in monosyllables), they just observe the world around them silently and helplessly. Their silence is a source of great unease for us; in fact, it becomes a judgement on our indifference to their plight. It is as though they are pronouncing us guilty, condemning us for staying silent through most of their struggles. It is the silence of centuries that often screams through the pages of the novella, so much so that language becomes a mere pretext for filling the void, a way of keeping a tenuous hold over our sanity, a way of staying alive in the face of this pervasive silence, which is as eloquent as it is nightmarish. Indeed, it is this interplay of silence and language that could be said to have become the marker of Gurvinder Singh's film, too. It is as though in his film version, Gurvinder has entered into the ontological experience of the novel and deconstructed it from within.

Another characteristic of this novella is that it strikes a near-perfect balance between the 'inside' and the 'outside'— the inner space of the characters and the outer space within which they are located. An alternate rhythm is set up in the novella; the first scene is set indoors, providing a close-up of the inner, private lives of Melu's family, and then it moves outside, where the inexorable cycle of oppression becomes operational, especially with the multiple intrusions of social reality into their private lives. The stark contrast between the private and the public space is one of the defining features of this complex narrative. In fact, the narrative is structured around multiple forms of 'binaries'. Binarism is built into the structure of the novel for two reasons; one, because all efforts at structuring a literary universe/cosmos derive meaning from this very principle, and two, because the social universe of this novella is not only oppressively hierarchical, but also antagonistically oppositional.

It is for some of these reasons that this novella could well be described as a 'cinematographer's delight'. Gurdial Singh appears to have envisioned it in terms of extremely evocative, powerful visual images, which constitute the language and grammar of cinema, too. In an imaginatively powerful manner, Gurdial Singh has captured in his language, the fragmentary images from the lives of several Dalit families residing in the village. Though these images are portrayed in all their painful fidelity to detail and characterization, it is Melu's immediate family, torn between the conflicting claims of the village (in which they were born and which has now abandoned them) and the town (to which they migrate and which refuses to accept them), which becomes the focal point of the narrative.

In fact, Melu's story is what one may refer to as the 'macro-narrative' within the novella, which otherwise consists of several 'micro-narratives' that form the mish-mash of its structural pattern.

There are five different 'frames' that constitute the narrative aesthetics of *Anhe Ghore Da Daan*. Unlike some of his other novels, which operate at both macro and micro levels, *Anhe Ghore Da Daan* is primarily a cluster of micro-narratives, with an overarching macro pattern holding them all together. These five frames occasionally overlap and coalesce, functioning somewhat like concentric circles, creating an eddying effect in terms of meaning and signification.

The outermost layer may be said to consist of the 'mythical frame', whose contours become visible once we realize the significance of the myth underlying the title. This myth has been derived from Pauranik sources, but significantly, the novel doesn't valorize or legitimize this myth; it simply subverts and critiques it. By thus setting up an ironic perspective on a cluster of micro-narratives interspersed through this novella, Gurdial manages to question the very basis of all macro-narratives and all hegemonic discourses on knowledge and power. Much of the poetic power the novella possesses also flows out of this mythical frame.

The second layer is that of the 'folk frame', the main bulwark of Gurdial's narrative. It is not the mythical story but its folk variant that structures the myriad events of the novel. Gurdial is conscious of the fact that 'myths' don't affect the lives of ordinarily people directly, but only through the mediation of 'folk consciousness'. For instance, the social custom prevalent among the rural Dalits of Punjab of going from door to door asking for alms, especially on the days of lunar and solar eclipses, is perceived as an act of distributive justice, an accepted norm in a paternalistic, agrarian, feudal society. Once the feudal network of relationships collapses, the need for such a system is also questioned. Here Gurdial's effort is to redefine the contours of this 'folk frame', for he knows that if it is even marginally shifted, the necessary space for consciousness-raising shall inevitably be created.

'Social frame' constitutes the third layer, which deals largely with a complex web of personal, social and economic relationships. Class-consciousness and caste conflicts, problems arising on account of the inequitable distribution of power, money and land, form the main dialectics of personal and social tensions in the novella. Gurdial Singh is fairly inclusive in the sense that he presents both the urban and the rural face of Punjabi society, complete with their attendant contradictions and dilemmas. Significantly, Gurdial Singh uses these social frames to demonstrate the complex operations of Foucauldian micro power centres, and the debilitating impact these have on the lives of the marginalized and dispossessed.

The fourth layer consists of the 'ideological frame' within which the ideas of justice, the coercive power of the state, the need for land reforms, the shifts in agrarian or urban economy, and the utter marginalization of Dalits in both the rural and urban milieus are examined and assessed. Towards the end of the novel, Gurdial Singh raises a very significant question about the utter hopelessness of Dalits. Melu's brother-in-law has escorted his sister and her children to town. Seeing their extreme economic distress, perhaps for the first time ever (as his sister had all along kept it a closely guarded secret), he is so moved that he asks, rather pointedly:

'But sister, if you have been in such dire straits here, why didn't you go back to your village?' he spoke, anger mingling with doubt.

'There in the village, it's not as though we are sitting atop a large heap of freshly threshed grain. Labour is what we do here, and that's what we are condemned to do there, as well. Even when we came here initially, it was not out of choice. For a whole year, he had been at a loose end; no one hired him as a siri. Besides, how can anyone live off their daily wages? In the village, you know, the daily wagers get only seasonal employment.' After a breather, she spoke again, 'Now, we are nowhere, neither here nor there. He is so weak and fragile that he can no longer work as a siri. So you tell me, where should we go?' (p. 65–6).

This response of Melu's bahoo keeps coming back to haunt the reader through the rest of the novella. Being a spectator, who simply observes her life from the outside and occasionally comments on it, bahoo's brother is virtually in the same position as the reader. Bahoo's brother is an insider (to the extent that he belongs to the same caste and class as Melu) and an outsider (to the extent that he doesn't understand the way things function in a big town).

The fifth frame, which I prefer to call 'human', is made up of 'individual micro-narratives' about Melu and his family, and other members of his community. Gurdial Singh ensures that right from the beginning we position ourselves with Melu and see his pain and the helplessness and tragedy of not-belonging from the inside. He makes us participate in Melu's life by inviting us to share his recurrent nightmare, in which he sees images of death and destruction, or monstrous animals charging at him, or a kite entangled in electricity wires, constantly buffeted around by wayward winds. In the language of narratology, this particular sequence is proleptic in nature, as it anticipates much of what the novella later goes on to reconstruct for us. Our main interest is not in what happens, but how it happens. By focusing on several Dalit stories, Gurdial Singh enlarges this frame, and by narrating them exclusively from the Dalit perspective, he defines his political position, too.

It would not be wrong to say that these frames function in the novella in much the same way in which a cinematographer would ordinarily use them in a film. As readers, we move across the spectrum of macro and micro layers of this complex narrative with perfect ease. These frames help us expand our vision when it is so required, and also contract or re-adjust our vision when we need to do so. It is almost as if the 'camera' is panning across with neutrality, sometimes giving us a long shot, and sometimes, a close-up. If Gurdial Singh's work is a cinematographer's delight, it is primarily because of his ability to conceptualize his novella in terms of these multiple frames.

Anhe Ghore Da Daan: The Novella and the Film

Film and novel are not only two distinct forms/genres, but each has its own set of rules and practices, its own idiom, language, even grammar. To my mind, when a film-maker chooses to make a film based on a novel, he doesn't simply borrow or adapt the given material in accordance with the constraints of his medium, he often innovates to such a degree that he ends up creating an independent, autonomous text.

Film and novella, should, therefore, be treated as two separate, discrete texts, which may become 'intertexts' for each other, but each must develop its inherent strength to stand on its own and also stand an independent scrutiny. In other words, as these are two distinct media, not only in terms of their language, grammar and structure, but also in the context of their reception and reading processes, it is important not to read one in the light of the other or to bring the experience of one reading to bear upon the other.

In the film, Gurvinder has not worked with a team of professional actors but instead used real-life characters, drawn from much the same background and milieu within which Gurdial Singh's characters often live their daily grind and struggle, before they die, unsung. Another reason Gurvinder Singh's film makes a powerful impact on the viewer is that he has been able to capture the distilled essence of 'poetic realism' that Gurdial Singh so consistently creates in his novels.

It is Gurdial Singh's finely honed understanding of the aesthetics of a novel that makes him a master craftsman. Gurdial Singh is a self-conscious writer, who is as mindful of the ideological concerns of his writing as he is of its aesthetic demands. He is one of those few writers in Punjabi who succeeds in attaining a precarious, almost delicate balance between the two axiomatic grids of novel/art, viz., ideology and aesthetics, something that Terry Eagleton would have us believe is the hallmark of all great writing.

Ordinarily, when we think about a film based on a literary work, we tend to treat the 'text' as the 'original' or the 'primary' or the *a priori* one, relegating the film based upon it to a 'secondary' or a 'derivative' position.

As a consequence, we begin to view the film through a textual haze, or gaze, which invariably becomes hierarchical, even hegemonic. In the process, we start comparing the two, and often enough, our effort is to point out how and in what manner the film is either a poor or a faithful adaptation of the novel, its qualified or unqualified subversion, or even a conscious deviation towards, or away from, the novel. In the process, we ignore a very important factor, which is, how the specificities of each genre demand a separate poetics of reception.

Even in its constitutive and cognitive processes, a film can never be merely a 'visual translation' of the verbal structure(s) of a novel. Regardless of whether a film is based on a particular novel or not, it constantly strives to become an autonomous, self-contained discourse. Under these circumstances, though it may be possible for us to emphasize multiple filiations between a novel and a film, textual gaze may often work to the detriment of the film and its reception.

Having said that, let me now address another related issue. If we are saying that it is not desirable to filter our experience of watching a film through the textual gaze, is it then possible for us to invert the gaze and approach the novel through a particular reading of the film? I do not know if such a possibility exists in other cases (as I have made no effort to test this hypothesis elsewhere), but I'm convinced that as far as *Anhe Ghore Da Daan* is concerned, it has been an extremely rewarding experience. Once I recognized the autonomy, separateness and distinctness of these two genres, absolving myself from the need to draw 'unholy comparisons' between the two variants, new 'structures of meaning(s)' began to emerge.

On watching the film, I realized that Gurvinder had made minimal use of words, relying more on the 'poetics of silence and space'. There are a number of scenes in his film where the characters just hang about and look helplessly on, refusing to articulate their subliminal thoughts. In the film, the gaze of the characters becomes a form of condemnation of the viewer, an expression of his guilt for not participating in their life processes. In most of these scenes, we see Gurvinder's actors passively looking on as the events unfold. This positioning of the characters as spectators, and not as actors, agents or participants, brings home the fact that most of them lack 'human agency' in the drama that unfolds before our eyes. With this insight, which I gained only through the mediation of the film, when I started reading the novella, it opened up a different perspective altogether. I could then see why Melu's bapu casts around helplessly in the novella, especially when his wife nags him or Dharma's kotha is demolished in front of his eyes.

In fact, the film moves smoothly between the polarities of words and silences, space and time, inner and outer, justice and injustice, rural and urban, landowner and landless, state and individual. Much of the structural tension of the film derives from the way in which the scenes are poetically arranged or, may I say, framed. 'Framing' is an important cinematic device that every film-maker uses to create his distinctive brand of 'poetics of cinema'. By using this framing device (already embedded in the structure of the novella, as explained in the preceding sections of this essay) to his advantage, Gurvinder has managed to create a multi-layered, polyphonic narrative, in which he is absent as an intrusive, controlling agent or as a dominant voice—a narrative that opens itself up, petal by petal, like the flowering of a lotus.

Conclusion

Over the years, Gurdial Singh's stature has grown far beyond regional, and even national, boundaries. His fiction has been so extensively translated into the English language that it is now possible for us to assess his work within the larger framework of world literature, something we could not have done earlier, when he was anchored within the limited domain of his own indigenous literary and cultural traditions. A proper assessment of Gurdial Singh's oeuvre is possible only if he is placed among the best of world literature available in the twentieth century.

If he learnt his craft of fiction-making (as he has often conceded in interviews) from such great masters as Gorky, Dostoevsky, Tolstoy, Chekhov, Steinbeck, Maugham, Hemingway and Irving Stone, he has emerged as a storyteller extraordinaire by virtue of the rich literary and cultural legacy he is likely to leave behind. If a history of world literature is ever attempted, I am confident that Gurdial Singh's name will appear alongside those of Chinua Achebe, Naguib Mahfouz, Gabriel García Márquez, Milan Kundera and Simin Daneshvar.

Rana Nayar
March 2016

Translator's Note

My association with Gurdial Singh's fiction goes back to 1991, when Pushpinder and I were commissioned by Macmillan (India) to translate his Sahitya Akademi Award-winning novel, *Addh Chanini Raat*. Since then, I have translated three of his novels and a collection of short stories. In 2012, I published *Gurdial Singh: A Reader*, which showcases the entire spectrum of his writings.

Before I delve into my experience of translating Gurdial Singh's fiction, I need to make a few preliminary observations about the specificities of Punjabi literature in general and Gurdial Singh's oeuvre in particular.

Right through its long, arduous journey, the tradition of Punjabi writing could be said to have maintained a vital, living link with a much older oral tradition. However, it is not easy to map this relationship as it has run its own distinctive course in the different genres available in Punjabi. Even without going into its intricacies, which would undoubtedly call for a much larger discussion, one may safely suggest that almost all Punjabi writers down the ages have tried to negotiate this oral/written, linguistic/literary space in their own distinctive manner.

However, in the case of Gurdial Singh, this particular

relationship takes on a very specific form; it surfaces as an unfailing insistence upon the spoken word. Being firmly rooted in the soil, he never fails to bring alive the natural rhythm and resonance of the spoken word. While this lends to his portrayal of situations and characters a rare authenticity and dramatic urgency, it also imparts to his fiction a certain quality of earthiness, even classical charm and simplicity. Largely recognized as one of the strengths of Gurdial Singh's art of fiction-making, it is this quality that may often turn out to be a major source of anxiety for his translator(s).

In my early encounters with Gurdial Singh's fiction, it was this challenge of having to render into English the speech of his rustic characters, with all its inflections and tonal qualities, that both enthralled and teased me. Had it simply been a question of finding English equivalencies for the local idiom used by his characters, it wouldn't have mattered so much. Translation, as any translator worth his salt would easily concede, is not merely a game of finding linguistic equivalencies at the semantic or the syntactic levels. Often the local idiom is so deeply embedded in the cultural layers that any attempt at a simple rendering could, at best, turn into a contraction or a reduction, and at worst, a deflection, if not a total loss of meaning. Besides, the syntactic structures in the two languages, viz., Punjabi and English, operate so very differently that often the process of transmission from one to the other may threaten to become obfuscating, even non-communicative.

Whichever way we choose to think about it, the loss is invariably of those cultural specificities that are intrinsically and inherently resistant to any act of translation, howsoever shrewd or strategic. While self-reflexivity is an inescapable fact of any translator's job, it doesn't always become a route to self-awareness. Even in those cases where it does become so, the practise of translation may often throw up challenges, which no amount of anticipation or awareness might help tide over. Faced with some of these limitations, the task of a translator, especially if he is seeking to capture the 'spirit of the original', may actually become all the more difficult, even formidable.

Often the 'purists' among the readers tend to question my translations on the grounds that they are heavily interlarded with the original Punjabi words and expressions. While some view this tendency as an expression of a lack of imagination or taste, or both, on my part, others choose to interpret it as an expression of my aesthetic failure, a desperate attempt to save the face by biting off the nose. All that can be said here is that in all translations of Gurdial Singh's fiction, long and short, I have consistently taken recourse to the original Punjabi words as a matter of conscious policy and strategy; not as the last manoeuvre to find a way out of the impasse. Kinship markers, forms of salutation, exclamatory words, and sometimes names of plants, trees, seasons, rituals and ceremonies, etc., are so deeply embedded in the specificities of the source culture that all efforts to render them into the target language prove self-defeating.

At this juncture, we ought to remind ourselves of Walter Benjamin's famous words, that not just translation, but rather all forms of writing are necessarily a deflection from 'the purity of the original'. Seen from this perspective, translation is never completely done in the target language, as is often assumed, but in what George Steiner describes as the 'third language' and often in what Homi K. Bhabha calls the 'third space'. If it is the search for the 'universal' in specific human experiences that makes translation possible, then it is the cultural specificity, often eminently untranslatable, that adds to the innumerable woes of a translator.

Hamstrung by such situations, a translator may find himself up against an impenetrable wall or an insurmountable cul-de-sac. Gayatri Spivak, an eminent critic and a distinguished translator herself (among other works, she translated Jacques Derrida's *Of Grammatology*), has pointed out the need to recognize the whole area of 'untranslatability' embedded in the archaeology of each seemingly translatable text. This is particularly true of Gurdial Singh as he often writes in what is popularly known as the Malwai dialect, which is heavily interlarded with local and regional specificities and therefore, is extremely difficult to render into standard English. What makes it all the more challenging is the fact that often, Gurdial Singh creates (as he does in *Anhe Ghore Da Daan*) a 'polyphonic novel' with a variety of registers, styles and voices. While translating different dialects into homogenized English, I have tried, as far as possible, to alert the reader about the distinctness of dialects by taking recourse to para-textual strategies. This is how I have tried to circumvent, or rather negotiate, the problematic area of 'untranslatability' while working on Gurdial Singh's fiction.

All along I have been conscious of the fact that far from being a mechanical activity (or simply a matter of finding lexical and/or semantic equivalences in two different language systems), which is how popular minds understand it, translation is a highly self-reflexive, political act. The politics of translation is inevitable in a situation where the source and target languages are as highly differentiated as Punjabi and English, even inequitably placed and distributed against each other in terms of their reach, spread, power and dominance. Being a dominant, global language, English is inherently privileged and if a translator, by accident or design, begins to collude in this process of domination by adopting a 'domesticating' rather than a 'foreignizing' method, the resultant de-culturation of the source language/culture is almost inevitable. And this, in turn, is bound to defeat the very purpose for which translations are often undertaken. By scrupulously adhering to the 'foreignizing' method and stubbornly refusing to make egregious concessions to English, not only have I tried to be partial to my own language, Punjabi (for which I am not in the least defensive), but I have also demonstrated the way in which my 'politics' essentially functions.

Though theorists like Lawrence Venuti have done their utmost to interrogate and problematize the much-abused notion of 'translator's invisibility' (there is an attempt to re-assert and establish the rights and prestige of the translators, something that history has stoutly denied them), I do believe that the translator is quintessentially a medium and not a source. If he has to find a new garment for the body of an old text, it is not only important for him to hide behind the skin and mask of the author, but also equally important to share in the worldview, perspective and/or ideology of the author. After all, the translator has to walk in step with another, tune into another's rhythm and grace and if possible, even create a world that is neither entirely his nor anyone else's.

Had it not been so, I probably wouldn't have returned to Gurdial Singh's fiction with the kind of unfailing religiosity that I have. Translating Gurdial Singh's fiction has been an eminently gratifying, though no less challenging an experience, for that reason. Perhaps it was so gratifying only because at every juncture, it threw up new and entirely unexpected challenges. His fiction has this unerring tendency to knock a translator completely out of his complacence. There is something about Gurdial Singh's fiction that doesn't submit itself readily to an act of translation, and least of all, to an English translation. In a way, the challenge is inherent in the fact that Punjabi and English do not merely represent two distinct, not necessarily antithetical, languages or linguistic systems, but two different cultural worlds as well.

All odds notwithstanding, if I continue to translate Gurdial Singh's fiction, it is only because across the barriers of age, time and space, I somehow feel a deep sense of kinship and affiliation with him and his work, which is as hard to explain as it is difficult to decipher. Perhaps it has something to do with the Punjabiyat we have inherited or a common dream we both share, albeit tacitly, that we must ultimately leave this world a better place than we found it; he, through his stupendous creations, and I, through my naive attempts at translating them.

Rana Nayar
March 2016

Anhe Ghore Da Daan

Tête-à-tête

It was a freezing winter night. The cold outside seemed endless, but inside lay steeped in a long, sprawling darkness. Crouching near the dim light of a deeva, two 'unhoye' were wrapped up in their own intimate chat. Tayya Bishna was narrating an ancient story to his nephew, Maghi.

'When the devtas and the rakshasas took sides in the churning of the ocean, one of the ratnas they managed to churn out was the nectar. The rakshasas were the first to get hold of it. The devtas started preparations to wage war against them. Just about then, a miracle happened, when Vishnu bhagwan, disguised as Mohini, suddenly appeared on the scene. So ravishingly beautiful was she that everyone was completely dazzled. The rakshasas, too, were mesmerized. Handing over the pot of nectar to Mohini, they said, "Now it is entirely up to you to do whatever you wish to." Mohini said, "Since both groups have played an equal part in the churning, both have an equal right to it." The rakshasas agreed.'

'So bhai! Mohini started distributing the nectar among the devtas first. One of the rakshasas, in the guise of a devta, sneaked in and sat among them. The moment he partook of the nectar, both the Sun and the Moon, seated on either side of him, recognized him and reported him to Vishnu bhagwan. Using his khanda, Vishnu sliced that rakshasa into two parts, but since he had already drunk the nectar, he didn't die. Converting him into Rahu and Ketu, Vishnu lodged both the parts permanently in the sky, and after finishing his job of distributing the nectar among the devtas, vanished from the scene.'

'Tayya, does it mean that the poor rakshasas were deprived of their share, then?'

Pretending to ignore Maghi's mischievous comment, Bishna kept up the tenor of his narration.

'Now, Rahu-Ketu became the sworn enemies of the Sun and the Moon. They say, bhai, that whenever there's either a solar or a lunar eclipse, it is nothing but an appearance of Rahu-Ketu, who come charging in, riding their chariot, pulled by blind stallions. They come back periodically, they say, to claim the share they were denied in the first place.'

'Share?'

Maghi's insolence had offended tayya to such an extent that he discontinued his story.

Maghi smiled. Peering hard into tayya's eyes, he said, 'All right tayya, just tell me, when will this conflict end?'

Tayya glowered at Maghi. Picking up an axe to cut off a few branches of a tree to light the chulha, he heaved himself up to go out, and as he did, he spoke in a harsh, grating tone, 'When you decide to end it!'

Maghi, too, was not one to rest easy. Following tayya, he said, 'All right then, I'll prove to you that I can actually settle it.'

Surprised, tayya turned around to look at him, peering to the left and right, but all he could see was the flicker of Maghi's grimy turban, swaying in the darkness that lay sprawling all around. Despite himself, tayya broke into a spontaneous smile.

As soon as Melu stepped inside the kothri, he shut the door behind him and went and lay down on the manji, without even bothering to put the light on. When he heard a sudden knock after a while, he got up with a start, mumbling, 'Who's it?'

Staring wildly at the door, he waited for a response but there was none. As he made an effort to heave himself up, he broke into a cold sweat. He felt as if the strength was ebbing from his limbs; so turning his back to the door, he lay down again, this time, his head resting towards the wrong end of the manji. For quite some time, he lay there, weak and dispirited, his eyes tightly shut. On opening them, he found himself face to face with a frightening spectre flickering on the wall opposite; the shadow was that of a kite cut loose, entangled in a mesh of electricity wires. As the kite lay hung, limp on one side of the electricity pole, its shadow was clearly visible, peeping out of the small holes and crevices in the wooden planks. The razor-sharp wind had blown holes through the waxed paper of the kite, leaving its bushy, long tail, like the fluff of a grimy cloth, hanging from the skeletal frame. (Even though he had known it for over a month-and-a-half now, each time he set his eyes upon this shadow, his heart would almost jump into his throat.)

When the tension became almost unbearable, he got up and came out of his kothri. Removing the lid and adjusting the earthen pitcher up against the wall, he poured himself some water in his cupped palm, and drank. Slithering down his elbow, the drops of water formed a small pool by his feet. Suddenly feeling the cold water about his feet, he sprang back in horror, almost as if he had stepped on a snake; and as he did so, the pitcher fell and broke into smithereens. The mud on the floor of the kuccha kitchen mingled with the clear water, turning it into slush. For a long time, he kept staring at the potsherds of the broken pitcher and then turned his gaze towards the bushy, long tail, the fluff hanging off the skeleton of the kite. Knotted up almost like a serpent, the bushy long tail was tossing freely in the wind. Stunned as before, he went back inside, and without so much as bolting the door, he lay down again, his eyes shut tightly.

Whenever such dread overtook him, sleep simply vanished. Even tonight, the moment he shut his eyes, it was as though something was trying to knock him out of sleep. And when sleep came fitfully, huge palaces and minarets, seven-storeyed, castle-like houses appeared to crash into ruins. Among half-broken walls, the twisted, gnarled girders of the roofs, the burnt-out beams and other debris, strange creatures, with heads of horses and torsos as big as an elephant's or a rhinoceros's would suddenly heave into sight, running amok in a wild frenzy. Standing back in trepidation and horror, hiding behind an uprooted column or a broken wall, he would stare fixedly as the demons went swishing around, raising endless clouds of dust amid the ruins…and then the thunder of the cannon balls would be heard, resounding all around. The dilapidated buildings would slowly vanish from sight, sinking into the haze of billowing smoke. And suddenly there would be a roaring crackle, a conflagration. And it was this menacing thunder of raging fire, reducing as it did a palace into cinders in the twinkling of an eye, which always shook him out of sleep. Inside the kothri, an all-enveloping darkness, overladen with swirling clouds of smoke, would pierce his eyes. He would feel his breath quicken, even become harder, and then he would sit bolt upright, staring abstractedly at the walls.

In the small hours of the morning, when some such dream jolted him out of sleep, he found it hard to fall asleep again. Sitting up, his chin resting upon cross-legged knees, he began to stare at the shadow of the kite. A sudden pain stabbed his heart, brining tears to his eyes. Closing them, he tried to fight back the intensity of the pain. At that very moment, he heard the sound of a cough outside. Exhausted, he lay down once again. The coughing became louder and more insistent. He felt as though it was his own father. (Around this time, in the small hours of the morning, his father would often start coughing, and this lasted almost till sunrise. His sides knotted up, the cough would get worse by the minute, so much so that he could hear his father's breathing get harder and heavier.)

After some time, this sound faded, and as it became increasingly less obtrusive, images from the past became sharper and clearer. There in the backyard of the house, upon a wooden manji lay his father, hamstrung by ceaseless coughs…

'Dyalo's bebe, it's time you got up and made a cup of tea for me…' Melu's bapu was heard saying, fighting to get his breath back; but unmindful of his pleadings, Melu's bebe simply turned over to the other side and went back to sleep.

Melu's bapu heard the sound of her breathing get lighter, yet he couldn't get himself to utter another word. (He was not in the habit of repeating his request a second time.) He knew that though she might take long to wake up, but once she did, she would immediately set about putting the water to boil, humming and hawing as she went about her work. As was her wont, even today she took her own time to get up. Pulling a khes over her shoulders and hobbling across to the chulha, she started grumbling in her characteristic manner, 'The firewood is soaking wet and so are the dung cakes...Do I burn the chulha with my head? No one is bothered about anything in this house...The young and the old are all alike...Each worse than the other...What do I do now?...Start cursing the ones I was born to...That too when the dawn hasn't cracked, yet?'

Melu's bapu knew only too well that any attempt on his part to intervene would simply add fuel to the fire. So, over the years, he had made it his practice to listen to all her recriminations in abject silence. Now, unlike before, he wouldn't allow rage to simmer inside, as his heart had somehow inured itself against it.

The cough persisted only so long as the tea wasn't ready. Having somehow managed to light the chulha with the same wet dung cakes, she now made a big fuss while handing him his cup of tea, and sounded so grumpy as if to say that he ought to be beholden to her for whatever she had done for him. Once through with it, she turned around, now to pour her venom upon Dyalo and Shinda. No sooner had they pulled themselves out of the bed than she stormed out, two or three rotis tucked under her pallu, and her work almost half unfinished.

'Bapu, where should I take the goats to graze?' queried Shinda, stoking the fire in the chulha as he downed his cup of tea.

Melu's bapu didn't react at all, almost as if he had failed to decipher the meaning of what had been said. Heaving himself up on the manji, he quizzed, 'Why? What is it?'

'In that grassland adjoining Mann's fields, they are running a tractor. And Dhillon's sons don't allow anyone to come anywhere near their fields…they say, "Your cattle stray into our fields and ruin our standing crop…"' Melu's bapu looked thoughtful. After a while, he gathered his wits enough to say, quite abstractedly, 'Take them to kassi for a graze, for a few days, at least. Then we'll see what is to be done. Do you hear me?'

'That new mate at kassi is really obnoxious. He snarls worse than a bitch. The other day, he started abusing us and, that too, without any provocation…He also told us, "Don't you dare come this way again…"'

'Doesn't matter! You tell him that it's only for a day or so,' Melu's bapu said, consoling him. But Shinda would have none of it. Then his bapu offered a sop, saying, 'You're a good son of mine. You shouldn't behave like this. Hang on till I recover. Then we'll go and sell our heifer at the mandi…And I'll take you to your brother in town…You can study up to seventh or so and pick up a job…Then you enjoy yourself. Look, it's only a matter of time…Let me just recover first…Do you hear me?'

This was certainly not the first time that Shinda had heard his bapu talk the way he did now. Somehow, he knew it in his bones that there was no escaping his fate. No amount of excuses, howsoever ingenuous, would either save the day for him or let him have his way. If anything, his excuses would only invite more rebukes, perhaps a severe thrashing as well.

Seeing the tension mount, Dyalo called him over to the courtyard on some pretext and then thrusting a thick lump of molasses into his pocket, she whispered, 'When you return I'll give you dried coconut to eat. I've put it away, especially for you.' Then handing him two rotis left behind by bebe, she spoke louder than usual, 'Now be a good brother of mine and get going. When I come to give bebe her roti, you wait for me near the peepul tree on the banks of kassi. I'll bring two rotis for you as well. And missi ones, if you like?'

Wiping his eyes dry with his kurta, Shinda groaned as he twisted the rotis to thrust them into his pocket before he spoke, his voice brimming with emotion, 'And if you fail to bring it, I'll refuse to go tomorrow.'

At first Dyalo couldn't help laughing at his childishness, but then a lump rose in her throat. Untying the cord of the young heifer, she-calf and the goats, she swabbed her face with her chunni and said, 'Don't, if you don't want to. But go, at least, now…Be a good brother, eh!'

Shinda slipped into a pair of old, worn-out, over-sized and pointed juttis belonging to Melu. As he stepped out of the courtyard, he first gave a stinging blow to the heifer upon its spine, and then brought down the same stick upon the she-calf's ankle, mouthing rough abuses. While the heifer and the she-calf, lifting their tails, took to their heels, speeding towards the fields, he stood there, his teeth clenched, his right hand wheedling the stick into the goat's 'things', and the left one rummaging through his pocket.

Melu's bapu had heard the sound of Shinda whiplashing the cattle. Dyalo knew it would have him worked up, so she shouted across to Shinda almost the way a town crier does, 'Weh, don't you beat these dumb ones!…They haven't had a bite of fodder since morning…And there you are, bashing them up, you fool!'

Unable to contain himself, Melu's bapu snapped irritably, 'This fellow is so stupid. Be it morning or evening, he is always crying. O bloody fool, don't you know how ill-starred we already are! It's like "O God, don't give me my daily bread, otherwise my mother will send me off to fetch the firewood." It's their evil deeds, perhaps; what a nuisance, they can't even think for themselves. O bloody fool, you think I'm rearing them just to bilk them one day? Even if we do make a little money on them, aren't you going to use it all up? Or do you think I'll carry it all away, tucked into my breast pocket...!'

Every time he was piqued by something or the other, he would fret and fume in much the same manner. When Dyalo heard him talk like this, she felt as though he was addressing himself not so much to Shinda as he was to Melu. Even though, deep inside, he felt terribly angry with Melu for not having maintained his link with 'this house' ever since he had left for the town, yet each time Melu came home on a perfunctory visit, that too, after a gap of four to five months, Melu's bapu would be euphoric for several days thereafter. What he found rather hard to contain was the sheer joy the thought that his son was living well gave him. After Melu's return, he would go around the village, spinning yarns and boasting,

'Now what should I tell you about city life! All I can say is that people really have a good time there. There's no interference, no nit-picking. You do your work, collect your wages and enjoy a good night's rest. There's no one around to grab your money or to make trouble. These mahajans don't trouble their workers half as much. In this respect, our jats are much worse. They flay you and glower. Now look at our Melu. He is enjoying himself. And what did he get out of that crop-sharing job he did for three years with these "one-eyed" ones. The sky above is my witness, and may God give me the strength to speak the truth. These people didn't give us even a single paisa. With great difficulty they parted with money, that too, not even half of what they owed us. And each time we went to settle the account, it was the same refrain, "You're the ones who owe us, not we you".'

But these 'stories' were for the benefit of other people. In his heart of hearts, he was sorely disappointed with Melu. Whenever Melu's bebe made the mistake of repeating this, saying, 'It's all right. They should earn for themselves and enjoy whatever they get,' he attacked her, saying, 'To hell with their enjoyment! We reared him, married him off, and even educated him up to class five. Now, we've to marry our daughter off. I'm unable to move my limbs. Isn't it his duty to save some money and send it to us? Do I get a regular pilshan that I can pay off all the family expenses?'

This invariably silenced Melu's bebe. Knowing well that there was an element of truth in whatever he said, she would, however, insist on passing the blame to her 'good-for-nothing' daughter-in-law, who, according to her, had perfected the art of inventing alibis ever since she had started living in town. Somehow, she always felt that her son was blameless, and that it was the daughter-in-law who squandered all her son's money on whatever caught her fancy, the soft-on-the-palate chaat or the fashionable clothes.

Walking in, Dyalo asked, 'Bapu, if you're feeling hungry, should I cook for you right away?'

But before Melu's bapu could respond to her, he was racked by yet another paroxysm of coughing. Without waiting for a response, Dyalo had started pouring flour out of the old container.

That very moment, Dheeru chowkidar came rushing in, holding a rough stick, panting and shouting, 'Oye, is there anyone alive here?...Hurry up...on your feet. Bloody, there's deep trouble there, and here you are, coughing away like a horse...You'd better get there fast...The panchayat has already been summoned...Oye, they've killed our people...!'

Melu's bapu couldn't make head or tail of what he heard. Though Dyalo shouted after Dheeru, he had, by then, already retraced his steps. She could only shout across to him in a tremulous voice, 'Tayya, why don't you tell us clearly what has happened?'

Without coming to the point, he simply shouted across to her, 'That is something you can find out later. Right now, you just send your bapu across. Tell him to hurry up.' And he went away, mumbling, 'You'll know what's happened once you've to pick up all your belongings and move to some godforsaken place like the gypsies...'

This was enough to make Melu's bapu rise to his feet. Wrapping the khes about his shoulders, he said, 'Putth, you get on with your kneading, while I go and make enquiries. This bloody fatso is making such a noise early in the morning.' As he slipped his feet into his juttis, ready to leave, he mumbled to himself, 'Hope nothing untoward has happened! It is rather unusual for him to sound so nervous...'

Barely had he gone as far as the polling-booth dharamshala, when he ran into Pala. Striding on ahead, his hands locked behind his back and his head and face half covered with an old blanket, Pala spoke as nervously as Dheeru, 'Oye come along. Why don't you walk a little faster? This time around it's not going to be all that easy. We'll have to rise to the challenge, whether we like it or not. How can we sit quietly over it? Today, "they" have been ruined tomorrow it could be "us"...'

Walking on ahead, Pala kept talking to himself as he went past a low, damp, fertile patch and cut a corner to head straight towards Wadhawa's fields. Hearing him speak, Melu's bapu felt as if someone had pushed him from behind. He stopped awhile, and adjusting the blanket around his shoulders, darted a quick glance all around. But for the three or four children who were busy playing, he couldn't spot anyone near the dharamshala. A cold shiver ran up his legs as he muttered, 'Oh my God, it appears the worst has already happened.'

Going across the fertile patch when he threw yet another glance towards the dharamshala, it appeared completely deserted. The women had left for the fields to gather firewood, chaff, green fodder or whatever, some perhaps to pick cotton; and all the men, it seemed, had retreated to Naranjan's arbour.

With the intense cold of January lashing against them, the tahli and keekar branches had begun to wilt. In Surjit Singh's fields that lay ahead, the wheat crop standing amidst the stubble of cotton had grown to the size of an outspread palm. Towards the right, in the adjoining fields, the sarson shoots, spreading as far as eyes could see, swayed majestically in the wind. The yellow flowers had acquired a brighter tint in the glow of the rising sun. Seeing it, Melu's bapu felt as if he was turning oblivious to everything else, at least momentarily, lost as he was in the shades of yellow and green that enveloped him.

Once again, it occurred to him that he, too, should set off towards Naranjan's arbour, but as soon as his eyes fell upon Pala's grimy turban heaving above the sarson shoots, he was seized by a sudden fear. Pala had walked on ahead, leaving him way behind. To think that 'the old Pala', who was perhaps no less than fifteen or twenty years his senior, was still as young and sprightly as ever, he was overcome by a sudden sense of shame. Though his own body was no less stronger than a lamb, he would often go hopping like a grasshopper.

'It's nice to feel reassured, after all.' Thinking about him, Melu's bapu muttered to himself, 'All his four sons were earning and all of them respected his authority, too. They brought him no less than thirty to forty rupees a month. With everything going his way, why won't a man at seventy or seventy-five prance around the way he does?'

As he looked up, the ground beneath his feet appeared to slip away. Beyond Naranjan's sarson fields, close to the far end, he could see an assembly of about fifty people. On peering harder, he saw a huge mud door where Dharma's kotha had once stood, and this was a long way off from Wadhawa's fields.

Not until had he reached the pathway skirting Wadhawa's fields did everything fall into place. But at that very moment (perhaps because of a sudden draught of wind) such a shiver ran through his body that his teeth began to chatter. And when he lowered the blanket over his head and face to wrap it around tightly, it triggered another bout of coughing. Right up to the bridge that lay over kassi, the spasm made him helpless. On reaching the bridge, when he raised his eyes, he was left gasping. No remnants of Dharma's kotha were visible; only the loud wails of Dharma's wife and daughter-in-law could be heard, mingling with the heart-rending shrieks of their children. When he heard a mix of voices rising from Wadhawa's fields— which were not very far from the pathway—from the people gathered there, he felt a strange dread rising, spreading and casting its shadow all around.

When he was about to reach the spot, it was almost as though he had been struck deaf. Their noise was now a deafening roar, like the sound of hail crashing down upon the reeds growing wild on the banks of a pond. Staring ahead with unseeing, vacant eyes, he couldn't recognize anyone present. On being pushed from behind, he stumbled forward to settle down on his haunches near a heap of mud. The village panch of their street, standing in Dharma's backyard, was busy proclaiming, apparently in a bid to soothe everyone around him, '...Now this is what we should do...without losing any more time, we should head straight for the DC's office. If he avoids us, then we shall go to the commissioner.'

'You may get into this "knocking about" later. First, you should think of how to put their belongings together and where to keep them?' Pala, the old one, intervened, glaring at the panch, 'Their hungry children have been crying for food since last night...And there are these people, busy giving a religious discourse...Wah! What sort of men are you, really?'

'O you, Tau of mine! All this has already been sorted out. You have turned up only now in the afternoon and started acting like a high priest!' The village headman glowered as he spoke.

Dharma's entire family insisted that they would not move out; they would rather stay on the rubble of their demolished kotha, without touching even a morsel of food. It seemed as if they had made up their minds about committing slow suicide. The panch of their street and other elders were of the opinion that the matter should somehow be settled amicably, at least temporarily, believing that a good deal of restraint was needed to handle the whole situation. But Dharma simply refused to concede. Rising to his feet, he announced his decision to the panch, 'O you youngsters, you may do what you please, but we shall not move from here till our last breath. As it is, no one can say that we are alive anymore. With the roof over our heads gone, our plight is much worse than that of the dead...'

With these words, he turned his back and walked away, leaving some fifty-odd men standing there, totally transfixed. For a long time, none of them were able to think of anything to say. The ageing Pala was the only one who had the courage to pick up the strands from Dharma. He started admonishing everyone, 'It's all right then! You think it'll help settle the dispute anyway? You've been talking so carelessly for far too long. And where has it led us? Has anyone bothered, even once, to offer a cup of tea to their children? All you can do is blabber endlessly, as if wisdom is all yours...'

Pala's reprimand did have a chastening effect on everyone present, at least temporarily. As a matter of fact, it hadn't even occurred to anyone that Dharma's entire family had not eaten anything since the previous night. If they had not made any arrangements, it was only because no one had any idea as to what had transpired, not until daybreak.

'I'll tell you what you must do,' the panch said philosophically. 'All of you should proceed to the dharamshala. There we'll take a decision and then proceed... Is that all right?'

Unable to accept the panch's proposal, more than half of those who had assembled there began to murmur dissent. There was the same crackling sound again, but seeing that there was hardly any other way out, all of them began to slink away to the dharamshala.

Up until now, none of them had turned their attention towards Melu's bapu. Sitting quietly, he was watching Dharma and Pala march towards Dharma's family, perched atop a small mound. As if on a sudden impulse, he rose to his feet and started towards them. On drawing close, he saw something incredible: the place where, until yesterday, was the site of two mud-plastered kothris, adorned with the utensils owned by Dharma's daughter-in-law, today was just a heap of loose earth, a foot-and-a-half-high. Two or three loosely tied bundles lay upon the heap. Among other things, some earthen pots and pans, utensils, old weeding implements and worn-out sickles, two shovels, the handle of a hoe and a handful of keekar branches to be used as firewood had been dumped in the middle of a wooden manji. Two of Dharma's granddaughters and a grandson were circling the manji, running around barefoot, dazed and frightened. Off and on, they would wipe their eyes clean with their shirts, look around bewildered and break into loud, heart-rending wails. Dharma's wife and daughter-in-law made no effort to console them, as they were sitting like professional mourners, their faces covered, almost as if they could not see or hear anything. They seemed to have been crying silently.

Some two or three feet away stood a solitary mud door. Beyond that, far off, near the city, rose the sky-high, demon-sized chimneys of the thermal plant. Intimidated, he turned his gaze away and moving closer, as he looked at the bundles and rags lying upon the manji, he felt as lost as a vagrant.

Dharma and 'the old Pala' had, in the meanwhile, moved over to the other side and were seated next to the iron poles upon which they planned to fix barbed-wire fencing. Dharma was sitting with his head bent, and Pala, who sat facing him, seemed to be handing down homilies in his characteristic manner. Melu's bapu came up and quietly settled down on his haunches, some two or three feet away from them. Both looked up momentarily, throwing a casual glance at him; then Dharma returned to his former posture and Pala went back to his homilies.

'Now this is what you should do—pack off the small children with me, at least till such time as any decision is taken. Treat our house as your own, or you think there is any difference between us? You and your two sons should adopt a do-or-die approach, pick up the lathis and stay put where you are…We'll see, how any "bastard" plucks up the courage to come anywhere near us…O my! Isn't it gross injustice…You've been here for seven years now…If it comes to that, tomorrow the village people will start saying "Bhai, this place where you all are living belongs to the village. Pick up your stuff from here and move over. We're going to demolish your kothris in the street and reallocate the land". And you think if anyone is ruined like this, he would simply get up and leave? Even if we were to agree to leave, where would we go? Is there any place we can call our own? People who have spent a lifetime here, wearing out their bones, where should they disappear now, leaving their homes behind? Eh!'

Dharma listened to him quietly, without nodding assent even once, all the while crushing the mud-baked bricks between his palms. Around this time, Dharma's grandson, who was probably no more than three, came and hid his face in his lap, and started staring at Pala and Melu's bapu, rolling his fingers in his mouth all the time. Wiping his eyes clean with a corner of the khes, Dharma pushed him aside gently. Crestfallen and dejected, he rose to his feet and walked away, looking over his shoulder, again and again.

As he looked at the swollen eyes and tear-stained face of the boy, Melu's bapu's defences crumbled. His eyes turned misty and when he wiped them with a corner of his turban, it was soaking wet.

Pala was still insisting on the same thing. Turning a deaf ear to him, Dharma asked Melu's bapu, 'How is your son, the one who lives in town?'

'He's all right. May he live happily, regardless of where he is!' Melu's bapu replied in an emotion-choked voice. Silent for a while, he shot a question at Dharma this time, 'How did all this come about? How did this misfortune befall you overnight?'

'Now, bhai, how should I tell you what happened?' Dharma replied, eyes downcast. 'It's nothing but destiny. That's the way they put it, I suppose...'

Before he could complete his sentence, Pala turned towards Melu's bapu and snapped, 'Do you live in this village or elsewhere? Say it? O you fool, it's been months since this trouble started and you want to know what the matter is? That's well said—I must say!'

But Dharma, as indifferent to Pala as before, turned to Melu's bapu and spoke, in a rather subdued voice, 'We've been here for the past seven years. Wadhawa Singh entered into a secret deal with Gopal Singh and sold off these sixteen acres of land to some factory owner. All we said was that we should be allowed to make an alternative arrangement, only then would we shift out of here. But last night, those factory owners came and pulled down our mud huts. Not just that they also walked away with some of our belongings. We did raise a loud protest, but who bothers? Did anyone come from the village to help us...?'

'Where were your sons, then?' Melu's bapu asked, surprise mingling with despair as he spoke.

'They have been in jail for the past five days. But now the very people who did that seem to have had them released.'

'Why?'

'Now how do we answer this, "why"?' Pala intervened once again. 'If someone says that "your beard shakes while eating", what explanation can you offer for that? Those people simply wanted to ruin them, and they knew quite well that if it happened in the presence of his young sons, it would create trouble, even lead to a brawl or something. So they got them arrested on the charges of possessing two bottles of liquor and a pistol, which had obviously been planted. Now as you know, for people like them, this is not difficult to do with support from the police.'

Melu's bapu couldn't think of anything to say, completely unaware as he was of all these goings-on.

That moment, they saw a jeep racing down the recently tarred road. Whizzing past the mound of earth, it turned left and drew up where they sat. Then speeding through Surjit's fields (the ones that had been levelled out after the harvesting of the cotton crop), it came rushing towards them. All three of them simply stared wide-eyed, fear lurking in their eyes. Even the women and children turned their attention towards it. Whirring up clouds of dust, the jeep came through the fields and pulled up near a dyke, beside a huge beri.

That very instant, all of them stood up straight, but Melu's bapu simply hung around, his arms locked behind his back. Dharma and Pala tightened their blankets around themselves. Stepping out of the jeep, three people came towards them, silence dogging their steps. A tall, strapping sardar, with a long, curling moustache was walking ahead. Two fellows were bringing up the rear, one slightly plump, striding confidently while running his fingers through his oily hair in a bid to settle it; and the other was kicking up huge clouds of dust as he walked. The latter was a thanedaar, a man of average height. Three constables too stepped out of the jeep, and as soon as they did, they began brushing the dust off their clothes and adjusting their belts.

'Why, tell me, bhai, of you three, who is Dharma?' Spoke the plump sardar as he came closer, peering hard at all three of them with his light-brown, cat-like eyes.

'It is me, janaab.' Dharma responded.

'And these two?'

'They are from my community, janaab.'

'Bhai, you both get going. I say, just scoot from here.'

Pala and Melu's bapu, too confused to react, just backed away a step or two and stood rooted, their arms akimbo. The officer glowered at them and said, 'Do I speak Pashto? Didn't you hear what I just said?'

'Janaab, they aren't here to carry "your" stuff away.' It was Dharma rather than the other two who spoke in a somewhat acerbic tone, 'They belong to my community. And they must share my joys and sorrows.'

'It is this kind of solidarity that makes you people lose your mind. Left to yourself, you would have settled this problem long ago, isn't it?'

'We don't even have a mind, janaab. You can lose your mind only if you have one.'

Rather than respond to Dharma, the officer once again turned towards Pala and Melu's bapu and spoke with the same authority as before, 'Didn't you two hear me? Go and sit under that keekar. Once I'm through with him, you can console him whichever way you want.'

Without demur, Melu's bapu proceeded towards the keekar tree. Pala too followed him reluctantly, muttering to himself as he went. Rather than walk towards the keekar, he settled on a dyke nearby. Melu's bapu obediently went off to stand under the keekar tree.

'So, bhai, what have you decided now?' The officer fired this question, his legs placed wide apart. Feeling his moustache, he twisted it on the left side with the fingers of his right hand. Hollowing out his left cheek and peering over his moustache with an almost-squinting left eye, he said, 'You'd better remove all your knick-knacks from here right away. And if you don't have a house to move to, a residential plot could be allotted to you. You'll also get some subsidy to build a house. And if you do own a house, make sure you make your way there quietly. If you try and act tough, then we know how to "soften" you up. Do you understand?'

'He has his own house in the vehra, janaab.' When the thanedaar, who was standing right behind the officer, stepped forward and spoke up, Dharma saw that he was the same man who had arrested his sons and led them away.

'Why, bhai?' The officer's voice had a strange menacing tone to it.

'Janaab, we have been living here for the past seven years. We did have an old, dilapidated kothra. When we came here, we used up parts of it to build this small tenement. Now, tell us, where do we go?' Dharma spoke in such a gruff manner that the officer's brown, cat-like eyes immediately began to smoulder. For a while, he just stared at Dharma, fixedly. Then casting a fleeting glance towards his left and right, he spoke in a voice harsher than before, 'Are you out of your mind? Do you know who you are speaking to?'

'First you arrested my sons. Then, you razed my house to the ground. How do you expect me to be in my senses, janaab? Only Jagjit Singh or you, janaab, can be in your senses.'

'Janaab, this fellow has always been very insolent.' Stepping forward, the thanedaar spoke up in an unusually stentorian manner.

'Don't you worry!' The officer spoke as though with clenched teeth, 'As they say, "When the dog snarls, it's not at you, but at your master!"'

'Where are the masters, janaab, who will protect us?' This time round, Dharma, too, spoke in riddles the way the officer had spoken. 'If we had someone to protect us, janaab, things wouldn't have come to such a pass.'

This time, the third person standing next to the officer spoke up, 'We have been pleading with you for more than two months now, that you make some other arrangements and leave us to our devices. And if you wish to get your face smeared with more dust, then do tell us. Now who is at fault, you or we?'

Tucking in the loose end of his grimy turban, Dharma stared at the man, who now stood talking to him in a rather familiar tone, for he had not seen him before. He couldn't even understand what the fellow was trying to hint at.

'Barely a hundred-yard-long rope and that too, knotted at one end.' The officer's voice was harsher than usual, 'Either you carry your stuff away by the evening, or I'll come around again, perhaps, the last time...Then I'll see how you refuse to vacate this place. Do you understand?'

'You have done your worst, already. And as far as the question of smearing dust on the face is concerned, I think it should be done to all those who first tempted us into moving here, all because they wanted to bleach our bones dry, and having done that, they are now asking us to vacate this plot, measuring less than five hundred square yards. Or let the dust be smeared on the faces of all those who couldn't put the barriers fifty yards away, and instead chose to demolish our kothas today. Not just that, they've also taken away all the wood, even nuts and bolts; perhaps, because they need it all to burn down their own havelis.' After speaking in this gruff, aggressive manner, Dharma suddenly fell silent, as though out of breath, or as if he had choked on his words. When he tried to tuck in the loose end of his turban that lay hanging off his neck with his tremulous gnarled hands, the officer once again hollowed out his cheek as he caressed the left side of his moustache. Then he twisted around to look at the third person accompanying him, as if to say, 'Now, you say, what is to be done?'

'There is no way you can force us to vacate this land. You may throw all our belongings in the field close by, but once you leave, we shall return. As long as justice is not done by us, we won't budge from here.' Wiping his eyes, Dharma spoke in a subdued tone of resistance, as though he were declaring his final verdict.

That very moment, the glowering officer announced his verdict as he turned towards the thanedaar and said, 'All right, SI Sahab, if this is the way it is, then let things be settled right away. Throw all the utensils and clothes a hundred yards away from the pillars, and then I'll see how they bring their stuff back again.'

'All right janaab.' With these words, the thanedaar turned back, signalling to his constables to execute the orders of the officer.

Looking fixedly in their direction, Dharma's wife and daughter-in-law were perhaps waiting for this very moment. Both of them heaved themselves up, dark fears looming large in their eyes. Seeing the thanedaar and the constables approach, the children, who until then had sat huddled close to them, now burst into loud, heart-rending wails, as sudden as they were persistent. Their screams of 'hai baba', 'hai bebe' and 'hai bapu' had now begun to pierce the atmosphere, making it somewhat sombre and fearful, once again. But Dharma just stood there, like a stolid pillar fixed in the earth; his hands locked behind his back, his eyes downcast.

'Hurry up, bhai. Finish the job.' The officer signalled to the constables, and then along with the other fellow, whom he had beckoned in a somewhat gruff voice, he marched towards the jeep, and started looking in the direction of the newly tarred patch of road. Pushing the wailing women aside as the constables were carrying a manji stacked with utensils towards the keekar where Melu's bapu stood, another jeep hove into sight, approaching from the left side of the track loader. It too pulled up next to the first jeep. A contingent of five or six constables got out this time, and the havaldaar who was accompanying them, hurriedly walked up to the officer and saluted him. Still lost in conversation with the other fellow, the officer simply signalled to him, with a wave, to go towards the thanedaar.

After sharing a word with the thanedaar, he returned and then signalling two of his constables to follow him, he proceeded to the place where Dharma's belongings lay scattered. Within no time, they gathered all that was left there, and threw it away under the keekar tree. Muttering all this while, Pala was first seen pacing up and down restlessly, pleading with the constables, and then, he was heard admonishing Dharma's wailing daughter-in-law and children to shut up. But it seemed as though none were prepared to pay heed to him.

By now, Dharma's wife had started beating her chest in despair, and each time she did so, she let out the name of one or the other relative of Surjit or Wadhawa, hurling mouthfuls of curses upon them all. Dharma's grandson and his two granddaughters stood clutching their sobbing mother's clothes, howling intermittently at the top of their voices. Unable to contain the irrepressible fear exploding inside them, it was as though their eyes were about to burst, with tears streaming down their faces.

Then Pala and Melu's bapu started walking towards Dharma, ever so slowly. After throwing all the stuff away, the constables, havaldaar and thanedaar proceeded towards the jeep for another round of instructions, after which the officer went off to sit inside the vehicle, along with the man accompanying him. As soon as he was seated, the jeep reversed and then clambering up the mound, it hit the road.

That very moment, the thanedaar ordered the havaldaar and his constables to arrest Dharma. Two of the constables stepped forward, pushed Dharma aside, and then gripped him by the arm to walk him along. As Dharma was walking demurely along with them, one of the constables suddenly muttered a filthy abuse and gripped Dharma's arm, giving it such a twist that he nearly lost his balance. Then God knows what came over them that they suddenly held both his arms and started dragging him along, as if he was just a dead dog. And then they sped towards the jeep as if they had stumbled upon a game. Pala, too, ran towards the jeep, shouting and screaming loudly, 'Oye, don't do this to him! You, O respectful ones! Don't be so cruel… Oye, God above is watching you! Just think of his family. Have some mercy on them.'

But much before Pala and the breast-beating women of Dharma's family could even run across to the jeep, it had already been reversed and was on the road. All of them were left behind, watching helplessly. Next to the pillar from where they had dragged Dharma away, Melu's bapu was standing, transfixed, his eyes gazing fearfully at the trail of Dharma's prints, left by his feet as he was dragged.

It was as if everything was over in the twinkling of an

eye. Turning back, Pala began to console Dharma's wife and daughter-in-law in a weak, dispirited voice, 'Have some patience...have patience. Keep quiet, now. Don't worry, God above is watching it all. You go and sit next to your belongings. We'll go to the village dharamshala and discuss everything with the panchayat. Moreover, I'll arrange for some food and ask my daughters to deliver it here. You'd better look after these children now. If you give up hope, it won't help. Don't worry! God will do justice by us. Don't be foolish, this is not the end of the road!'

For some time, Dharma's wife and daughter-in-law continued to sit alongside the trough made by the wheels of the jeep, crying and wailing loudly, and then, on their own, they wiped their faces with the edges of their chunnis, and started collecting and assembling their scattered belongings.

Walking across to Melu's bapu, Pala spoke in hurried tones, 'Come on, bhai, let's go. You'd better walk fast now.'

And walking ahead of him, Pala kept talking to himself compulsively, though Melu's bapu remained unmindful of it all. All he could see ahead of him was the long, deep trail left in the ground by Dharma, as he was dragged along. The loud wails and howls of Dharma's wife, daughter-in-law and children had now become a constant buzz in his ears. Tightening the blanket around himself, he raised his head, and saw that the sun now hung a little above the keekar on the mound in Surjit's fields. Though the fog had melted away a bit, the sharp rays of the sun had only made the chill a shade worse.

'Paliya, what is going to happen now?' Melu's bapu asked as they neared the pond, as though the seriousness of it all had sunk in, just then.

'What will happen?' Pala spoke as if he was still lost, 'Don't worry, you simpleton. They can't hang him just like that. They can't, henh? Now when the entire panchayat goes and presents a petition to the DC Sahab, he will have to respond to it, no? He can't just turn us away. Henh! You tell me this, will he just rebuke us, and send us all packing? What right does he have to ignore the will of the panchayat? These days, the panchayats have a lot of rights. Why won't he listen to us?'

Melu's bapu felt as though Pala was just shooting his mouth off, because whatever had to happen had already come to pass, and now no one was going to pay much heed to whatever they had to say. As this thought crossed his mind, a cold sigh escaped him and he cast a glance, straight ahead, at the dharamshala, where all the members of the panchayat, including the panch had gathered inside, and were busy talking loudly to each other. Sidling up to them, Pala started narrating everything to them, right from the very beginning.

For some time, Melu's bapu just stood next to the platform outside the dharamshala, looking stunned, and then he returned home, as dazed as ever.

'Dyalo, bhai, do you have enough dough for five–six rotis?' He asked in a dispirited voice, as soon as he entered.

'Why, what's the matter, bapu?' Dyalo asked, surprised, 'Do you want me to make rotis?'

'Hanh! Their children are crying of sheer hunger. If you were to make a few rotis, I could go and give them to the children.'

While lighting the chulha, when Dyalo heard someone's footfalls outside, she turned around and saw a woman dressed in a new pair of clothes, a long veil drawn over her face, stepping into their house. Dyalo recognized her instantly. She was Melu's bahoo. Bringing up the rear was her brother, a huge bundle resting on his head, and in he walked along with two of her sons.

'Sat Sri Akal, massra!' he said, as soon as he walked in. 'What say you? Henh, are you well?'

The moment Melu's bapu set eyes upon him, he simply kept staring, so completely befuddled that he couldn't even respond to his 'Sat Sri Akal' in a proper manner. That very moment, Melu's bahoo first touched his feet and then after scratching her feet against the chulha, where Dyalo sat, she walked into the kothri. Her brother, too, followed her in, and leaving the bundle inside, came out, and spoke again, in the same booming voice, 'So, massar sian, are you well?'

'Yes, I'm strong as a heifer.' Melu's bapu first glanced at him and then looked around, 'Why don't you pull that manja down? So, how is everyone at your end?'

'Hanh very well, with your blessings!'

Settling on the half-baked bricks lying next to the trough, he said, 'I was going to drop bibi. No bus, so we thought of coming here. I said, "Let's meet our massar and the rest of you".'

Melu's bapu lowered his eyes. He had a fair idea that at this age, people hardly knew how to conduct themselves. On peeping into the kothri, he felt as though bahoo and her children were in hiding somewhere inside. Feeling a strong urge to shower his affection on his grandsons, he asked in a weak voice, 'Dyalo, my child, have Leelu and his brother already gone inside?'

Long before Dyalo could respond, bahoo's brother called out to both of them, 'Aao, oye, you town-boys, your baba is looking for you.'

But the boys didn't step out. Feeling sheepish, bahoo's brother walked in, and catching hold of their arms, pulled them out. With their fingers stuck in their mouths, they stepped out, feeling diffident. They came and stood guiltily in front of their baba. Melu's bapu first made them sit next to him, and then wrapped them up in his blanket. But the moment he saw them wearing torn shirts, pyjamas and rubber chappals, his heart sank to his feet.

'Massar, these boys have really become very naughty,' bahoo's brother spoke again, as he took his seat on the same bricks. 'Living in town has really made them very clever, but in their studies, they are still laggards. They get marks only for tearing up their books or breaking their slates and ink pots.'

This comment had barely diverted the attention of Melu's bapu for a split second, when both the boys, slipping out of the blanket, ran back into the kothri. After a while, they came back out, chasing each other. They ran towards the backyard and then went rushing out of the house.

'Look at them, they are really wild,' bahoo's brother spoke, glancing in the direction in which they had gone. 'Not even for a minute do they stay home. There too, they leave before the crack of dawn, their pockets stuffed with marbles. And return home only when the last cock starts crowing. Their aim is so perfect that no one can ever defeat them at the game. Both return home, having won seven sugarcane sticks each. And this happens almost daily!'

Melu's bapu saw that the boys had gone off towards the dharamshala. He was no longer paying any heed to what bahoo's brother was saying, as he was staring in the direction in which his grandsons had gone. Bahoo's brother kept talking, as if to himself, '…Massar, now all of you should also join them in town. Melu was saying that by the time his children return, he'd have rented out a spacious house. I told him that he should go in for a good one. Pucca and two-roomed. There are some very good houses in that locality, which have come up on the road leading to the town. Melu was saying that even the rent is reasonable. And if he has already rented one there, well, so much the better. All of you can enjoy life there.'

Pausing a bit, he continued, 'Massar, I too am thinking of settling in the town. You get good wages for your labour and you earn enough to eat well. Nowadays, our jats are more miserly than the banias. They don't let you take anything for free. They squeeze every last drop of lassi they give to the siri. So mean! And if earning money means working your butt off, then why should we take nonsense from anyone? Now the jats are no longer what they once were—you can't utter so much as a "hai", even when they do a real good job of flaying you alive. In the town, at least, you get money in your pocket on a daily basis. Here, they skin you alive for more than six months, and then say, "Wait for another month. Let me marry off my son, and then I'll settle your account"… As if it is a question of thousands and lakhs. Look at them! They expect us to hold on to their tails, and be dragged along behind them. Only if someone were to ask them, "Don't we too have stomachs to fill…?"'

Melu's bapu was familiar with bahoo's brother's tendency to continue blabbering for hours together. Ordinarily, he would come to their house only to pick up bahoo, or drop her back. He had two older brothers, but they rarely visited as both were buried in domestic chores. Besides, they were much more reticent and quiet by temperament. One of the reasons why it was always he who was asked to accompany his sister was because being 'a carefree bachelor', he was still dependent on his father.

'Dyalo, bhai, have you made the rotis?' Melu's bapu was

suddenly reminded of Dharma's family. But the very next moment, he spoke in a feeble voice, as though something had occurred to him all of a sudden, 'Once they are ready, call these boys indoors and feed them. Put a piece of molasses on their roti... I'm sure, they have had nothing since that one meal in the morning.'

'Why massar, before starting from home, both of them tucked away two rotis each. No wonder they are spinning around like potsherds. Else by now, they would have been hovering around the chulha like moths. They are not the kind to miss their meals, ever.'

'No, my dear, it doesn't take children very long to digest what they eat.' This time round, Melu's bapu spoke in a somewhat testy voice, 'And in cold weather, children tend to feel very hungry. Winters are more like smouldering kilns, you know.'

While making rotis, each time Dyalo stole a glance at bahoo's brother, he would stare back at her, rather brazenly. Earlier too, every time he came to their house, he would lose no opportunity to take potshots at Dyalo. Not that they had ever spoken much to each other, but somehow Dyalo could never warm up to him. Being short and dark-skinned, he looked more like the saddle of a bullock, and barely reached Dyalo's shoulders.

'Bapu, I've made the rotis. You, too, have some.' Along with her bapu, she invited bahoo's brother to join them. Making excuses, bahoo's brother tried to evade the issue, saying, 'Massar, I have already told you that we ate long before we set off from home. It is wintertime. Unless you eat, you can't beat the cold. Well, if anyone is still hungry, let him eat.'

After garnishing the roti with a slice of pickle, Dyalo added a piece or two of molasses to it, and then thrust the thali into the hands of her bapu. Ignoring the repeated pleas of bahoo's brother, Melu's bapu literally forced the thali into his hands, and then walked out, in search of his grandsons. By the time he returned, Dyalo had convinced her bharjai, too, to have at least one roti. Once they were back, the boys, too, went ahead and had a roti each. But Melu's bapu refused to eat, saying, 'I'm not hungry, yet.' Wrapping up the three rotis she was left with in a kitchen napkin, Dyalo put them in an alcove in the whitewashed, kuccha wall.

'Bapu, what about bebe's roti?' When Dyalo popped this question, Melu's bapu suddenly turned reflective.

'Massar, do people of this village offer chaa-roti to the winnowers?' asked bahoo's brother, in a bid to draw Dyalo into the conversation, indirectly.

'When the winnowers aren't available for the job, they are even willing to pay twice the amount. On top of that, they make generous offers of chaa-roti, too. But now this practice has become so rare; these days, they don't even settle the wages.'

'I know this world is really very selfish. When people need you, they don't mind even owning up a donkey as their fufhar. Otherwise, they refuse to even recognize you. Our village is also like that.'

Seeing his naivety, Melu's bapu couldn't help smiling to himself. A twisted smile danced on his lips, as he spoke, 'Bhai, your village must be in another region. And there, perhaps, God himself is different.'

When bahoo's brother started asking Melu's bapu questions about the people assembled in the dharamshala, his attention was suddenly drawn towards them. The sounds of uproar could still be heard coming from there. When he had gone to call his grandsons, Pala had shouted out to him, asking him to return immediately; for they might all have to go to town. Now mulling it over, he stood up and said, 'Dyalo, bhai, I'm going to the dharamshala.' Then looking towards bahoo's brother, he said, 'You people take it easy. Let me go there once, and see what is happening. Henh?'

'Massar, we too, shall leave now. What will we do, sitting here?' said bahoo's brother, rubbing his slightly twisted fingers over his shining, razor-thin moustache, 'If I miss the second bus also I won't be able to get back before evening. As it is, the people for whom I work as a siri don't let me get away for an entire day. Like the Angrez, they account for every hour and minute.'

'So you are leaving? So early? Why don't you stay overnight? And leave early tomorrow morning?' Melu's bapu suggested this with the idea of spending a few affectionate hours with his grandsons. He wanted to discuss so many things with them about the town, their new house, and their studies. So far, they had just been scampering in and out of the house, feeling somewhat sheepish and self-conscious, and hadn't even spoken to him properly.

'No.' This time round, bahoo's brother spoke rather firmly, 'Go we must, but if you insist, we'll delay our departure a bit.'

Melu's bapu peered inside the kothri, hoping that bahoo might say something about delaying their departure, but she said nothing. Ever since she had gone in, she hadn't stepped out even once. So Melu's bapu spoke in a somewhat diffident tone, 'All right, bhai, it's entirely up to you, we won't force you.'

'No, massar, there is no such thing. If I had my way, I'd have returned to the village without a moment's delay.' It was as if bahoo's brother was on the back foot now, offering a weak defence of his position; but without paying much heed to his words, Melu's bapu had quietly sauntered off towards the dharamshala.

The people assembled at the dharamshala had decided that all the people of the vehra should go and discuss the matter with the DC, at least once. The chowkidar had been packed off to summon the sarpanch and other panches, but so far, none of them had turned up. The chowkidar had been to their houses twice; and still none of them had come. Nor had anyone given a straight answer; all they had said was, 'We'll be there in a while', and then forgotten all about it.

'If they aren't coming, why don't we go and call them. It's not going to sully our feet, anyway. Come on, let's all go to the house of the sarpanch,' Pala said, in a bid to flaunt his wisdom.

Some of them dug in their heels saying that the sarpanch must be summoned to where they were, but then on the insistence of a few wise ones, all of them started for the sarpanch's house, though somewhat reluctantly.

When twenty to twenty-five men, wrapped in their old, musty and torn chaddars and khes, started towards the sarpanch's house, dragging their worn-out juttis, making clouds of dust whirl behind them as they walked sullenly, it appeared as though some inexplicable, potential threat hung in the air. Men and women, busy around the house, left whatever they were doing, and came and stood in their doorways, staring at them as if they were dacoits of some kind. The children playing in the streets or running in and out of the houses looked at them with fearful eyes; but no one had the courage to ask them anything. They, too, stared at the walls and doors of the village as though they were marching through the streets of some unknown, alien village. Seeing tension writ large on their rugged, weather-beaten, sunburnt faces, the village people, felt as though they had never seen them before. The dishevelled beards on their faces were more or less the same colour as the soil—neither black nor white; it appeared as though the dust of their ancestors' beards had also mingled with theirs. Their eyes had the same vapid, vacant expression. It was as though a strange, inexplicable, pallid fear hung over their heads; and the same fear also lay curled up around the street.

Walking through the streets of the village, they reached the house of the sarpanch, facing the west. Seated in the courtyard, he was busy talking to some people. In a courtyard spread over a kanal-and-a-half, the sarpanch sat on a high-backed chair, and the people sat all around him on a large manja. All of them wore juttis woven with silk threads, and had thick, woollen chaddars wrapped around their shoulders. Their ivory-coloured, starched, tall turbans signalled that they were all from the majha region. One of them, cloaked in an expensive pashmina shawl, held a double-barrelled rifle. Two of them had shotguns, and two of them carried long, sheathed kirpans; their impressive bearing creating an impression that they actually belonged to respectable families.

Seeing so many people outside his door, the sarpanch hurriedly slipped on his juttis, adjusted his blanket over his shoulders, and then spoke in a voice louder than usual, 'I told the chowkidar that I would be there soon. Why did all of you take the trouble to come so far?'

No one replied. Walking closer to the threshold of his big-framed, main door, he spoke, somewhat defensively, 'Tell me, what's the matter?'

The panch from the vehra, who was standing right next to him, edged closer to him and asked, 'You mean to say, you don't even know what the matter is?'

'Naa bhai.' Looking much more defensive than before, the sarpanch spoke, 'I'm ready to swear by whosoever you want that I have absolutely no idea what it's all about. The chowkidar is standing right behind you. Ask him, bhai, if he has told me anything?'

Balancing his weight on his staff, the chowkidar stepped forward a little and then spoke in a somewhat edgy tone, 'Bhai, sarpanch sahab, is this something new that you don't know about? You talk as if you are a little child, henh? It's been nearly two months since this trouble broke out.'

'Oye, you crazy one, there are so many "problems" in the village, this is not the only one.' It was as though the sarpanch wanted to wish away the entire matter. 'Every second day there is trouble of some kind or the other. How could I possibly know what kind of problem you were asking me to intervene in?'

All of them fell silent. Looking at their faces, the sarpanch stood rooted to the ground, feeling decidedly odd. After having waited in vain for their reply, he said, 'Anyway, let it be. Don't create a mountain out of a molehill, but tell me straight away, what is the matter?'

Then the panch started explaining the matter to him in 'straight' terms. 'Dharam Singh had two kothas on the land that was sold to the factory owners by the three families of Surjit Singh recently. The factory owners have razed those two kothas to the ground.'

'Razed…them…to…the…ground?'

'Razing them to the ground, they have even carried off the logs of wood they dug up from there,' the panch spoke somewhat peevishly. 'When we went to the dharamshala to discuss the matter, they even had all the little knick-knacks thrown out of the demarcated boundary. Moreover, the police has arrested Dharma and taken him to the police station.'

'Really?... Is that so?' The sarpanch spoke in a subdued voice and then stood with his eyes downcast.

Two persons, who were earlier sitting on the manja close to the sarpanch, now came and stood next to him. One of them, who, despite his advancing years, appeared to be stout and of moderate height, stepped forward and as he did so, swung the butt of his double-barrelled rifle around, in a bid to save it from hitting against the frame of the main door. Then, covering its open mouth with both his hands, he spoke, leaning forward, 'Sarpanch sahab, we know much more about this trouble in your village than you do. Let me give you the details. We met Jia sahab, last night. He was the one who told us the whole story. You understand?'

All of them looked at that man, including the sarpanch. Around the edges of his ebony-black eyes a ring of red glowed, smouldering like fire. His pink, broad forehead seemed to shine beneath a carelessly tied loose turban. His grey hair, shining amidst his thick, bushy beard and moustache, appeared to lend a special charm to his glowing face.

'Jia sahab was telling me,' said he, clearing his throat and then continuing, 'that the land on which this fellow "Dharma-Dhurma" was illegally sitting had been sold to the factory owners for something like one lakh twenty-five thousand rupees. This fellow Dharma started saying that since my kotha is built on this land, you give me whatever compensation is due to me. They told him, bhai, you give some evidence to prove that this land belongs to you. Now, where would he get the proof from? He could have given proof only if he had bought this land out of the "pounds" his father gave him. Jia said that so far they had been looking towards the panchayat, but now they would go in for a legal action…and this is what they did. Now this is the long and short of it. These matters don't relate to the "territory of some king" that you claim not to understand them at all. We know it despite being a third party and you claim that you don't, despite being the insider. This behaviour on your part is rather strange!'

After speaking in such a spontaneous manner, he suddenly fell silent and looked at them, as though waiting for a rebuttal. For a while, everyone just stared at him. Then, fondling his beard, he cleared his throat once again, and said, 'In practical matters such as these, we shouldn't create any obstacles. At this rate, tomorrow, I may claim that this house of the sarpanch also belongs to me just because I once had a meal here… That means, the law has no meaning whatsoever, and what prevails is "the rule of my father". After all, brother, it's not the law of the blind that operates here. Or does it?'

'It is the law of your father, after all.' A short person, who was standing next to him, adjusted his shotgun as he spoke, 'When our so-called leaders have got dharamshalas built for themselves on the shamlaat land, just to be able to secure votes, got taps installed, appointed their boys, who never study beyond primary school, as officers over our heads, then why won't their rule prevail? Now, you and I or the sarpanch don't really matter.'

The moment the sarpanch heard these sarcastic words, he felt as though they might trigger a minor revolt. Turning his attention away from both the men, he looked in the direction of the panch from the vehra and said, 'Look, all of you leave immediately. I'll first go and contact the other panches and lambardars, and ask them to come along with me. We'll follow close on your heels. You go and wait near the shack of the village lawyer. Then, we'll approach the DC. What do you say?'

'How long do we wait for you there?' the panch asked, his words dripping with distrust.

'Why would you wait at all? I'll be there before you arrive.' The sarpanch spoke with a tone of finality in his voice, and then in a bid to reassure them about his keenness to accompany them, he said, 'I just have to slip on my juttis. I'll follow you, close on your heels.'

Then signalling to those two men from the majha region to move inside, the sarpanch turned his back on the group and walked off. Those two men kept looking over their shoulders, smiling somewhat meaningfully, and followed the sarpanch indoors. Transfixed, all of them just stood there, rooted to the ground until the panch signalled to them to move on. They returned to the dharamshala like they had left it, feeling somewhat like 'a band of aliens' in their own village.

'Look brothers, now you'd better listen to me carefully.' On returning to the dharamshala, the panch spoke in a firm and composed manner as though he wanted to hammer a point home, 'Don't have any illusions about our getting justice as soon as we reach there. And you'd better be clear about the meaning of each word that that majhail spoke at the sarpanch's house. We also know that the land on which Dharma's kothas were built actually belonged to Wadhawa and his ancestors. But don't forget, Dharma's family was uprooted from the village and forced to settle there by Wadhawa, as he wanted his orchards to be guarded. They were the ones who built these kothas for them. In the presence of the entire panchayat, they vowed that "from now on, this entire piece of land measuring a kanal-and-a-half shall belong to Dharma and his family". But all that was part of an oral agreement. What has happened now is something legal. If such legal actions become the norm, then all of you better get ready to move out of the vehra, bag and baggage. The entire stretch of land that is now called vehra actually belongs to the villagers. Even if you were to look through hundred-year-old documents, you wouldn't find your names or those of your ancestors' there. The land documents in possession of the patwari clearly suggest that all this land once belonged to the king and, according to the law, is now held by the government. It's entirely up to the government to accept your ownership over it, or that of the village. But legally, you have no right over it.'

After a while, he looked at their faces; all of them looked withered, just like a bunch of crushed acacia flowers. The defeated look in their eyes had acquired a new earthy tint. Seeing all of them stare at him in a rather awkward, unsettling manner, he felt as though he needed to launch his final lecture. 'Now, you listen to my advice. If we succeed in securing the release of Dharma and his sons from the police, and somehow manage to get back possession of that piece of land for them, then you may say that we too get a hearing within this system. Otherwise, tomorrow, they may throw us out, bag and baggage... So you must know how to protect yourself.'

'How can we leave the village and go?' Getting to his feet, Pala spoke as though he wanted to challenge him, 'You talk as if you just want to scare us off. Henh? You simpleton, if we've been in possession of these houses since the times of our grandfathers or great grandfathers, then how dare anyone uproot us from here?'

'Have patience, chacha! Have some patience.' Signalling to him to sit down, the panch made a gesture as if he was trying to calm him down, and said, 'I have only told you the legal position. After all, even Dharma had possession of the land that belonged to Wadhawa Singh.'

'These evil ones, they can't loot so much.' This time round, Pala sounded testy. 'At this rate, these people won't even allow us to use their fields for defecating. What kind of a law is this, bhai? You go around pretending to be a big chaudhary?'

'According to the law, even today, they can stop you from entering their fields. And there is no way you can challenge that.' The panch was as composed as before.

'Then what is this fuss all about?' Jumping to Pala's defence, it was Ghudha who spoke this time, 'What kind of a leader are you? You are the kind who always says: "Oye bebe, the day I become a thanedaar, the first thing I'll do is break your ankles". Wah, bhai, wah! Shabaash!'

'Oye, you people have a knack of twisting things. Tell me, if I bring you to ruin, where would I go?' This time, the panch was somewhat agitated, 'I have always believed that the law is only for the powerful. Haven't we always said, "With the powerful, even 'seven scores' equal a hundred"? If you are powerful, then the law is on your side; and if someone else becomes more powerful than you, the law becomes their chattel. What does it have to gain from you, jet streams of milk from the udders? As they say, "the buffalo belongs to the one who wields the lathi", no?'

The panch, in fact, was in the habit of saying such strange things to his people, but no one had ever understood what he meant. But today, God knows why or how, despite the doubts raised by Pala and Ghudha, the people were listening to him intently, as if they understood every word he uttered.

For a while, the panch continued to explain his viewpoint.

Finally, they all came to the conclusion that at least eight or nine of them must go to the district courts with him, meet all the big officers they could, discuss the matter with them, and if they didn't succeed in finding a way out of the crisis, they must return by the evening so as to be in time to convene yet another meeting to determine the future course of action.

Soon after, the panch, Pala, Ghudha, Miru and three other persons left for the town. Of those who were left behind, some sat down to share their 'wise schemes', while others went back to what they were doing earlier.

As Melu's bapu walked back from the dharamshala, he felt as though his entire body had been turned into a gunnysack full of loose earth. All the vehra houses appeared to be desolate and deserted to him, as if no one had ever lived in them. Looking at those houses with puzzled eyes, when he came closer to his own, he felt, perhaps for the first time ever, that he was going to enter 'someone else's house'. The place through which he was passing was not a regular street, just an odd-shaped vacant lot, which measured barely four hands at places, and, at others, nearly four feet. Not even a foot's worth of space was even or regular. As water constantly spilled out of their houses, the entire stretch was full of slush. All the people of the vehra, men, women and children, would often hitch up their clothes and look for a dry patch to step on, while going towards the dharamshala. But why hadn't anyone ever thought of levelling this place by shovelling some dry mud over it? As this thought flashed through Melu's bapu's mind, he felt a shiver run down his spine, as though a long-forgotten memory had suddenly returned to haunt him. But the very next moment, it occurred to him that this was a 'no man's land', so why would anyone think of levelling out this 'alien land'?

The moment he came in, he saw that both his grandsons were busy playing marbles in the courtyard. Seated next to the chulha, bahoo was engrossed in conversation with Dyalo. With his face down and legs akimbo, bahoo's brother was lying on the manja, next to the heifer's trough. At that moment, Melu's bapu really felt that he had walked into someone else's house. So much so, he even forgot to clear his throat audibly, the way he did whenever he walked into the house, as a warning to his bahoo to cover her head.

'Massar, we were waiting for you only,' bahoo's brother spoke, as he got up from the manja. 'Or we'll be very late. So, we'd better go.'

Almost like a stranger, all that Melu's bapu could get himself to say was, 'All right bhai, as you wish,' before he fell silent. Bahoo's brother walked across and picked up his bundle from inside the kothri. As bahoo got to her feet, she pulled a long veil over her face before leaving the kothri. And pocketing their marbles, the boys ran towards the dharamshala, ahead of everyone else. Dyalo walked up to the corner of the street, from where bharjai decided to send her back. With the idea of seeing them off to the bus stand, Melu's bapu continued walking with them.

As they came closer to the small pond, Melu's bapu twisted around to look at the fields of Wadhawa Singh. Dharma's wife, Surjit, and his little children were still sitting next to their luggage, near the keekar, as stunned as ever. He felt a strange sense of despair wash over him. With his eyes downcast, he stepped on to the mud dyke and started walking along it, unmindful of what bahoo's brother was constantly blabbering. As he walked, he kept staring at the grass blades, thinly encrusted with dewdrops.

As he neared Rama's fields, where the cotton plants still stood swaying, waiting to be harvested, he looked up towards the sun—it was at its brightest. Right in the line of the sun, on the ground, he saw the same track loader, now stationary. Its upturned loader, raised some three or four feet above the ground, looked somewhat like the jaw of a monstrous, elephant-like animal. He felt as though two or three persons were strolling on its higher ridge, almost the way in which lambs saunter around a raised mound. While he was watching, suddenly it produced a menacing 'grrhh-grrhh' sound, and its jaw began to descend towards the earth. Melu's bapu was so scared that he suddenly halted in his tracks. Even the boys, who were running on ahead, looked in that direction, and slowed down; but the very next moment, they ran off towards the road. Bahoo's brother kept up his blabber, as if he was busy talking to himself.

And suddenly, the track loader started slithering towards Dharma's kothas, making a rumbling sound as though it was dumping the wreckage into a big heap. Melu's bapu felt as though it was moving like a python holding its breath, and that it jerked suddenly, too, as it came closer to the uneven ground next to Wadhawa's orchards, before it sank its lion-like teeth into the mounds and mounds of loose earth deposited there. Its 'grrhh-grrhh' sound grew louder, far more menacing than before. Its huge mechanical parts seem to be moving jerkily, in much the same way as Meetu's knees often jerked, especially when he pounded sheets of iron with his calloused hands. With this jerky movement, the jaw of the track loader, already deep in the soil, began to sink even deeper.

Busy talking to himself, bahoo's brother had gone on far ahead. Slipping away from his side, bahoo, too, had hurried her steps to catch up with her brother, thinking that if they were to miss yet another bus, then they might have to wait by the roadside until the late afternoon.

But Melu's bapu was still looking fixedly at the track loader. Now, as it began to raise its jaw, lumps and lumps of loose earth started falling off its sides. Moving jerkily on the uneven ground, the track loader suddenly backed away, lowering its jaw, as though preparing for another head-on collision, the way a buffalo does. Through repeated assaults, it flattened the entire stretch within minutes, in the same way that a child makes a house by pouring wet sand over his one foot, and then kicks it off with another, levelling it all out. All the loose earth in its jaw was thus scattered all around. Melu's bapu lowered his eyes once again. But the moment he did, he suddenly heard the loud screams and wails of Dharma's wife, daughter-in-law and little children, almost as if they had been crushed under the weight of the machine.

A shiver ran down his spine as Melu's bapu looked towards the road ahead and saw a car and a jeep rushing past. He felt as though this particular jeep was in no way different from the one he had seen in the morning. The car went swishing past, but the jeep went screaming towards the chimneys of the thermal plant. As it sped forward its size began to diminish, and it gradually appeared to be as small as an ant.

As soon as bahoo and her brother had reached the roadside, they sat down under a keekar tree. Walking right in the middle of the road, both the boys had started dancing alongside and shouting, 'Bus has come...bus has come.' Their mother called out to them, reprimanding them severely and, asking them to return. Feeling scared, they had barely managed to reach the keekar, when a truck, overloaded with cotton bales, breezed past, like a maelstrom. Its thundering sound appeared to send tremors through the earth. As the thought, 'what if the boys had been run over?' hit Melu's bapu, he was deeply shaken.

As he approached, bahoo's brother shouted across to him, 'Massar, what is the frequency of the bus service on this route?'

In response, Melu's bapu looked at him as though he hadn't understood a word of what he had heard. But coming closer to the keekar, he spoke in a weak voice, 'Bhai, you never know. Sometimes they come after every half hour, and sometimes, two come together after two hours or more. Sometimes, not even a single bus comes until the evening—they have no fixed timings, really.'

'It's the same in our village, too,' bahoo's brother said. 'In those parts, one or two "privit" buses also ply. In these parts, I think, only the government buses run. No?'

'They are all just the same, the government and the private ones. It makes no difference in the way they function. It all looks to be the same. Without a ticket, you are not allowed on the bus anyway.'

Stepping forward, Melu's bapu sat down next to bahoo's brother, slightly away from bahoo, and started looking towards his grandsons, who had already gone towards the fields in search of bers, barely visible to the naked eye in the haze of dust that was blowing in from the irregular mounds. Seeing him looking fixedly in that direction, bahoo's brother, in a preemptive move, hollered out to the boys, 'Oye, why don't you both come here and sit down quietly? You, a dog's... What if you get run over by a truck or something?'

The boys got so scared that they immediately stepped off the road, went to another keekar a little distance away, and turning around, stood peering in the direction of the track loader. Bahoo's brother also looked in the same direction. He asked Melu's bapu, 'Massar, whose land is this—the one that is being levelled?'

'It belonged to three families, who jointly owned it, but it has now been sold. They say that some factory is going to be built here.' And then it was as if he could no longer rein in his emotions, 'That place, you see, on slightly raised ground, which they are now levelling out, is where Dharma from our vehra had his kothas. Last night, they razed them to the ground...'

'Razed them? How did they do that?'

Running his hand over his dishevelled beard, Melu's bapu said, 'Oye simpleton! Is there any way you can fight the powerful? All they wanted was to pull it down, and that's what they did... Right now, the entire family is sitting under the keekar tree over there. Who knows what all it may now lead to? The panchayat has gone to the DC. But let's see.'

'Now this is the limit. How could they do this? How could they pull down the houses people were living in?' Rising to his feet, bahoo's brother, in a bid to reassure himself, looked in the direction where the track loader was at work. Seeing a couple of women and children seated under the keekar tree, he was somewhat thrown off-balance and said, 'If this is the way it was, then why did all of you in the vehra play possum? You should have declared a war against them. In such cases, one shouldn't really bother about the consequences.'

Looking towards bahoo's brother, who, at that moment, appeared to be somewhat like 'a spindle of a spinning wheel', Melu's bapu said, 'You think we made no effort to sort this out?'

'You must have. But obviously, massar, these efforts were not enough to break anyone's leg.'

Melu's bapu felt as though bahoo's brother was criticizing

everyone in the vehra. In a bid to divert his attention, he looked towards his bahoo, and said, 'Bhai, Beero, my daughter, you must tell Melu to come and meet us, one day. So many things have to be sorted out. You know, I can't do any work now. The girl is waiting to be married off. And Shinda is still a child. So you see, now the entire burden is upon you all.'

'Don't worry, babaji, I'll send him as soon as I get there.' Pulling her ghoonghat up and down, and glancing at him sneakily, she responded in a firm voice, 'We always tell you to come there and live with us. That will end our worries, too. We'll make do with whatever little he earns.'

On hearing these words of bahoo, Melu's bapu was so deeply gratified that a lump rose in his throat. Clearing his throat, he said, 'Don't worry, baccha, we'll talk about this plan of moving there another time. But right now, you just send him over to us. We can't pack everything and leave so soon. Now it all depends on what God wills. That is what will happen, ultimately.'

He had barely finished speaking when they heard the rat-a-tat of the approaching bus. All of them rose to their feet. Admonishing the children, bahoo's brother asked them to come closer. Making a strange, roaring sound, the bus pulled up some ten yards away from them. With great difficulty, bahoo's brother pushed all of them in from the rear door, and threw his bundle inside. As soon as a man and a woman had disembarked from the front door, the bus heaved like a camel and started moving. It didn't allow Melu's bapu enough time to caress his grandson's heads, or his bahoo to touch his feet.

Turning his attention away from the bus, Melu's bapu looked towards the man and woman who had disembarked. Both of them appeared to be outsiders. Adjusting the cotton chaddar he had already wrapped himself in, the man asked, 'Lambardaara, we've to go to the sarpanch's house. Do we take this outer road?'

'Yes, this is the right one. Close to the pond, you follow the circular road, towards the left.'

Both of them went quickly down that road. This time round, Melu's bapu appraised them very carefully. The woman had covered her face and head with an orange shawl, just the way honey harvesters often do. It was difficult to say whether she was young or old. Her clothes and footwear were of the latest design. The man, too, appeared to be quite well turned out. He couldn't tell who they could possibly be; but much before he could untangle this riddle, they had already disappeared in the afternoon haze.

After a while, when Melu's bapu turned around, he was somewhat surprised to see that he was still standing by the roadside. Running his gaze all around, he felt as though everything had a strange halo about it. This road was just a kuccha pathway in the good old days, when he used to ferry Chanan's wheat grain and stuff to town. There used to be high mounds on either side. In those days, all that grew in these barren fields of Surjit and Wadhawa were wild, bristly bushes, or occasionally in the season of harhi, you'd get to see a few stray shoots of black gram, or some millet plants in the season of sauni. It would then appear as though seeds dropped by nature had taken root out of nowhere. In the middle of this wilderness, there used to be a mound as high as a kotha, spread over a small patch of land, measuring a kanal-and-a-half, where cattle would be left to graze at all odd hours. In those days though, things were not so bad, yet this piece of land did not yield enough harvest to pay for the taxes levied on it. But now the same land had been sold for as much as three-and-a-half lakhs; it was no joke. Everything appeared to be so strange, as though the entire country had become unfamiliar.

Then suddenly he thought of what his bahoo had told him about possibilities in the town, and this reassured him, easing his conflict-ridden state. With renewed vigour, he started thinking about the houses in the town's basti, where his Melu had probably already rented out a much bigger and a better house, and that from the bus stand, his daughter-in-law and his grandsons would ride their 'own rickshaw' to go to this new house...

On alighting from the bus, when bahoo's brother looked all around, he couldn't spot Melu anywhere. He couldn't see any other rickshaw puller, either.

'It appears as if Melu and others like him have gone on strike. Henh bhaine?' Bahoo's brother sounded rather crestfallen, as he lifted the bundle off the ground and put it across his shoulder.

Bahoo saw that there was not a single rickshaw on the road. Next to the wall of the bus stand, towards the town, a few tongas overloaded with passengers were waiting; but it seemed as though they were heading towards the villages in the vicinity.

Carrying the bundle on his head, as bahoo's brother stepped out of the bus stand, feeling somewhat troubled, he said, once again, 'What's come over my brothers-in-law, today? All of them seem to have gone somewhere and died, henh?'

They had barely turned towards the corner to take the road leading to the police station, when they heard slogans being shouted, rather loudly. As soon as they turned the corner, they saw that the rickshaw and tonga wallahs had blocked that entire stretch, right up to the market. Multicoloured cloths tied to long sticks had been placed atop all the tongas like banners, with all kinds of slogans written on them. Rickshaw handles, too, had flags attached to them. Two rickshaws, pulling up close to them, were, in fact, leading the procession. Two persons sitting in these rickshaws were carrying the tallest flags. One of them, who wore thick glasses and a trimmed beard, was now hoarse with insistent slogan shouting.

'Oh, sister, Melu must be among these people,' said bahoo's brother, stepping off the main road.

Grabbing hold of both her sons by their hands, Melu's bahoo, too, backed away a little before she added, 'Even if he is, he's not going to take us home in a "car". This is now a routine affair with them. I don't know what their problem is, that every five–seven days, they start shouting and congregating like this. Then they arrive home, sheepishly, their bones and bodies all bruised and broken.'

'Bhai, Bhai Singha, what is this commotion all about?' bahoo's brother asked a man who looked poor, dressed in a frayed coat and torn trousers, standing by a tea stall along a side of the road.

Giving him a fleeting, casual look, that man then looked towards the procession and said, 'What can happen to them? It's because they are so well fed that they always keep wailing. They are saying, increase our fare. Bloody fellows, as it is, don't you flay us alive? Even if you have to go to the bus stand, you ask for no less than two rupees. The rate is only seventy-five paisa, but they'll say, "Sit if you want to, or go your way." Now they are feeling the heat, as five or seven of them have been challaned. And that heat has now turned into a conflagration. Do you see why they are preening like crawling ants?'

Looking straight ahead, he continued to talk in this peculiar vein, as if venting his long-suppressed anger. When his words didn't draw the attention of even those who were standing right next to him, he slunk away into one of the streets, still muttering under his breath. Kick-starting his auto rickshaw parked some ten feet away, he reversed and sped away to an unknown destination.

'What kind of a thing is that, sister?' Looking in his direction, bahoo's brother asked in all innocence.

'Such people too exist here! Well, these are rickshaws that run on motorcycles. Damn them, as they are the ones responsible for the entire mess. Everything was fine till they hit the roads. Since then, our incomes have reduced by almost half.'

The procession had now inched closer to them. Bahoo's brother was keen to leave only after it had gone past them. He liked the idea of so many people together, lustily shouting slogans. Seeing them in action, he also wanted to join in and shout. But his sister was getting restless. Still, he kept stopping on the way to turn back and look at the procession. Going past the police station, the procession turned towards the bus stand.

'Really, sister, Melu must be in the procession. What if he has already shifted the house? Where will we go looking for it?' Angling for an excuse to watch the procession, bahoo's brother made yet another bid to stop once they were closer to the school. Seeing a huge crowd of youngsters assembled outside the school, all of whom had probably come to watch the procession, Melu's bahoo felt a tremor in her voice as she spoke, 'It was only the day before yesterday that he sent us this message. How could he have moved into a haveli, so soon?'

The long, serpentine row of rickshaws with flags was getting much longer. If he had had his way, he would have liked to have enjoyed this spectacle for some more time, but recalling his sister's harsh words, he decided to follow her rather demurely.

Reaching the basti in front of the mill, as soon as they turned into one of its narrow and wet streets, Beeto, the wife of their neighbour, Miana, the foreman, immediately stepped out of her dark, dingy kothri, and enfolded Melu's bahoo in an affectionate embrace. After making polite enquiries about her parents, and caressing the heads of the children, she literally forced everyone into her own baithak.

As bahoo's brother crossed through the narrow door, he shuffled the bundle from his head to his arm, and said, 'Sister, your doorway is very narrow.'

It was his first entry into this house. (Earlier, whenever he had come, he hadn't been able to stay long enough to either visit or know the insides of the neighbour's houses). On hearing him speak in this manner, Beeto first adjusted her pink voile duppatta over her head, and then flashing her glowing white smile, she said, 'Brother, after all, the doors can't be bigger than us.'

Bahoo's brother felt as though she had cracked a very serious joke with him. Quietly, he walked in and sat down on a manja placed towards his left, and seeing that it had a freshly washed bed sheet with painted red flowers spread over it, he put his bundle down on the floor.

'I'll be right back.' With these words, Beeto slipped through the back door of the baithak as though she had vanished into some dark tunnel.

Then appraising the baithak from the roof to the floor, bahoo's brother leaned a little towards his sister and asked her in a conspiratorial voice, 'Sister, do they own this house?'

'Why, it's a rented one, but in a way, it is as good as theirs.

Previously, her father-in-law lived here. After he died they have been living here for the past eight years. Neither can those people make them vacate, nor do they want to vacate it.'

'What would the rent be?'

'Not more than twenty or twenty-two rupees.'

'Twenty, twenty-two rupees? For this dingy room?'

'Do you think it's on the higher side? We pay something like twenty-five rupees. If they were to leave this room today, people would be willing to pay up to fifty or even sixty rupees, and yet beg them for it.'

The truth had not yet dawned on bahoo's brother. Surprised, he started peering at the half-naked women peeping out from the wall-calendars, and at the brass, copper, chinaware and silver utensils adorning a wooden shelf, and the three trunks in a corner. With great difficulty, two regular beds could have been squeezed into this baithak. The thatched roof was so low that he could have easily reached up and touched it if he was on his feet. Though it was still high noon, yet the room was dark. The foreman's wife had left a light on. The plaster was peeling off the walls, and a strange stink of dampness rose from the walls and the floor.

'What does he do for a living, sister?' asked bahoo's brother, leading her into a conversation.

Trying to listen to the hissing sound of the kerosene stove and peering towards the rear door, she edged closer to him and whispered into his ear, 'She says that he works as a "foreman", but he actually works at the grinding mill, over there.'

Bahoo's brother found this rather strange. He asked, 'But why must they lie about it?'

'That's how your stock goes up. People begin to think you are from a wealthy family.'

That very moment, Beeto walked in and asked, 'Brother and sister, first tell me if you'd like to eat something?'

'No sister. May God bless you! We had our meals before we set off. It barely takes us fifteen minutes from there. It must be half an hour since we started from home.'

'Please, don't hesitate. It's your own house, after all.' Sitting down on the manji next to them, Beeto asked the children, 'What about you, "the evil ones"? Do you want to eat something?'

The boys also refused by shaking their heads. Seeing this 'show of hospitality', bahoo's brother couldn't help smiling, so he immediately loosened a side of his turban and covered his face with it.

Beeto was wearing a dark red kurta and salwar. This made her glowing complexion bloom all the more. Despite being thickset, her youthful, healthy and glowing looks were attractive. Bahoo's brother liked her animated laughter—which brought the same freshness to her face that corn flowers blooming in the fields often gave off.

For some time, sitting there, she kept talking to them casually of this, that and the other, and then disappearing behind the rear door, returned with four cups of tea on an old tray. In the middle of the tray, she had placed a plate of pakoras and sweets. Settling the tray on top of the trunks, she pulled out a durrie lying on the manji, and spread it out in front of him. After putting the tray on the durrie, she walked out the rear door once again. When she came back, she had another cup in her left hand and the kettle full of tea in her right one. Settling the kettle on the shelf, she sat down on the trunks, facing bahoo and her brother, and flashed such a smile that even he turned crimson, and instantly lowered his eyes.

Bahoo's brother had liked the way she had gone in and out of the room; he gathered a little courage, he looked straight ahead and smiled back at her. Holding the kettle in her hand, Beeto was trying to persuade them to have some more tea, pakoras and sweets, all this while keeping up the flow of neighbourhood gossip. Listening to what all had transpired in the mill basti, while Melu's bahoo was away, bahoo's brother thought for a moment that everything had gone topsy-turvy. But the very next moment, he found himself staring at Beeto's blood-red lips from which streamed anecdotes and stories.

Who knows why, but bahoo's brother had somehow begun to like her already, though he had known her only for a short while. Looking at her hungrily, he started thinking, 'What if I, too, get someone like her...' But he couldn't complete this train of thought, as it snapped bang in the middle, like a delicate kareer twig.

After finishing her tea, when Melu's bahoo asked Beeto for the keys to her house, she said, 'I'll just look for them. In the morning, I think, he did hand them over to me.' After rummaging for the keys on the shelf, and pulling them out from behind the utensils, she handed them over to her and said, 'Look? Are these your keys?'

Melu's bahoo said, 'Our keys won't get so easily mixed up with others. Our lock is typically rustic and old-fashioned.'

Holding the bundle, when bahoo's brother bent down a little and stepped out, he felt as though he had come out of a dungeon. Looking back at it from the outside, he said, 'If we had such a door in our house, our children would have pulled it out by the evening, striking it repeatedly with their shoulders.'

'That's why we didn't get into the trap of having children, you see,' Beeto laughed heartily, stepping out with them. On hearing this, bahoo's brother was really surprised.

When his sister was turning the key in the lock outside her house, he asked in a somewhat mysterious voice, 'Sister, don't they have any children of their own?'

'Not really. It's been seven years. They have tried all kinds of remedies. But unless it's in your karma, nothing will happen. Isn't it?'

Turning around, bahoo's brother peered towards Beeto's door, but she had already gone inside. Seeing Beeto laugh such a matter away, he was quite surprised. This had made her all the more attractive to him. 'These town people are so fun-loving. They enjoy themselves…' he thought to himself, though this did not in the least lessen his curiosity about her.

'Oye, may I die!' As soon as Melu's bahoo had opened the lock and let herself in, she slapped her forehead and said, 'I don't see anything here. My entire house has been turned upside down. Where have all my utensils gone?'

Anxious, she started rummaging behind the manji that stood at a right angle against the wall.

Then she opened both the trunks and peered inside. She also swept her hand under the other manja that had been laid out. Seeing her overcome with anxiety, her brother said, as he put the bundle down on the manja, 'Do you think, your neighbour could have taken them away?'

'Why would she?' Melu's bahoo spoke in a tear-soaked voice, rummaging through the canisters and gunny bags lying around, 'Why would this poor woman ever do such a thing? This is the handiwork of…that same fellow who, as it is, has sunk my boat.'

'You mean Melu?' Sitting down on the manja in the midst of the clothes scattered all around, he asked in a nervous tone,

'Has he too started doing such things?'

Unmindful of his words, and still looking around the cramped kothri with the sharpness of an owl, bahoo suddenly sat down on the manji with a thud, as though her legs had given way under her. Then in a choked voice, she said, 'Had I known this, would I have left my house and gone?... Now it'll take him two months to buy all this stuff. What am I going to do the cooking with, his head?' Crestfallen, she sat down, and started wiping her eyes.

It was the first time that bahoo's brother had come to know of any such thing. He was terribly angry with his sister, who had until then, kept all this from them. So he spoke to his sister, half-chiding, 'Why wail your heart out now? You might as well put up with it. If you are not even going to confide your woes to a bhai or a bhabhi, then what is it to us...go and die a dog's death for all we care!'

Melu's bahoo couldn't get herself to speak even a single word in response. She was perhaps ruing the fact that once all the secrets of her household were conveyed to her parents and through them, to the relatives, she would feel all the more humiliated, even inferior. Wiping her tears, she spoke, with mild trepidation in her voice, 'Be a good brother, and don't you convey such things to anyone! We'll manage things the way they are. Why should we lend ourselves to social ridicule? No one will come to our rescue anyway.'

After a minute's silence, Melu's bahoo blurted out everything, saying, 'Bira, how can I possibly hide it from you. It's been the same ever since we came here. Sometimes, we go to mortgage four utensils or ornaments, and sometimes, we go to get them back. What else can we do? When income dips, how do we stay afloat?... Every other person wants to ply a rickshaw. When we first came here, there were around fifteen or perhaps thirty rickshaws; now there must be no less than a hundred. Under these circumstances, how can we earn anything?'

Yet, she had managed to conceal something important from him. Looking at her brother, who was now feeling more and more uncomfortable, with moist, tear-stained eyes, she said, 'He has no bad habits, no addiction. Once in a while, he might break his vow and drink just a little, that too, when he is in the company of others, but otherwise, he is the kind who advises everyone against it...and says things like, "Oye, you stupid fools, you work so hard to earn a little money, bleaching your bones in the bargain. And if you just drink it all away, it is like casting money into a well. Who would call you wise, if you do that?" But what can he do? When he doesn't earn enough through the day, then he goes for a night shift. His body is wasting away, and he hardly has any appetite left. It's been seven years, and not even a spoonful of desi ghee has gone into us. Not just our bodies, but our souls, too, are completely exhausted. When he comes home late in the evening, he says, "My legs are wobbly..." He doesn't even tell me everything. Who knows, he may have started taking drugs under the influence of others, or because he has to stay awake through the nights.'

Though bahoo's brother kept listening to her in silence, he felt as though she was simply trying to humour him the way you would a child. All this while, as he was listening to her, he kept thinking of Chanan, the one-armed character he knew in his village, who would always preach the same mantra to all the youngsters, 'One, don't ever confide in a woman, and two, don't ever trust her. Always remember this. A woman has more than a hundred faces, and being a fool, a man can't even know the secret of one. Then how can you ever know the secret of her hundred faces?'

'But sister, if you have been in such dire straits here, why didn't you go back to your village?' he spoke, anger mingling with doubt.

'There in the village, it's not as though we are sitting atop a large heap of freshly threshed grain. Labour is what we do here, and that's what we are condemned to do there, as well. Even when we came here initially, it was not out of choice. For a whole year, he had been at a loose end; no one had hired him as a siri. Besides, how can anyone live off their daily wages? In the village, you know, the daily wagers get only seasonal employment.' After a breather, she spoke again, 'Now, we are nowhere, neither here nor there. He is so weak and fragile that he can no longer work as a siri. So you tell me, where should we go?'

Though bahoo's brother had understood everything his sister said, somehow, his heart was unwilling to accept it. Then suddenly, he felt a strange tremor convulse through him, as though his perfectly healthy body was on the verge of collapse. In a bid to divert her attention, he said, 'Doesn't matter. Why give up all hope? So long as we are around, why should you worry about anything? You are really a simpleton. Aren't your brothers of some use? Are they meant to be rubbed on the carbuncle, then?'

Seeing her brother lavish so much affection on her, spontaneous tears pooled in her eyes and started streaming down her face. A lump formed in her throat. With great difficulty, she managed to say this: 'Shabaashe, brother! Who else is there for me, apart from you?'

'Now you tell me, do I need to go and get something

from the market?' Her brother spoke reassuringly, 'If you need money, take another five–ten rupees from me. Henh? Or I'll return to the village now. Why wait until dark?'

'Today, you stay back, henh!' Wiping her tears, she spoke with the same confidence her brother had instilled in her, 'Why come and leave in such a hurry? You haven't even had a glass of water in my house.'

'Look at you, you crazy one! Am I a stranger here? I would have stayed back, but bapu will worry unnecessarily if I don't go. Moreover, what will I do if I stay back today? Why waste a whole day?'

Though the fact that her brother had come only a little while ago and would leave very soon had pierced her heart like a thorn, all that Melu's bahoo said was, 'All right, then,' and fell silent. (As it is, she was scared that were he to stay overnight, several other secrets of her household might also tumble out of her heart.) When he pulled out a two-rupee note from his pocket to hand it over to his nephew, now playing out in the street, she held his hand firmly, and said, 'No, bire, don't do this. As it is, we have given you enough trouble.'

'I'm not giving it to you. I'm giving it to my nephews.' And with this, he forced the note down his nephew's pocket.

Her eyes turned moist all over again. Wiping her tears with a corner of her chunni, and caressing her brother's head, she said, 'You should have stayed back for a day, at least…'

But before she could conclude her sentence, her brother responded, 'Don't worry, it's nothing, really. It's not a hundred miles away. I had no idea about your problems. You never shared them with us. Or else, I'd have come here off and on. Now, I promise, I won't be lax; I'll come after every five or ten days.'

Both the boys walked with him to the street corner. He

bought them sweets for twenty-five paisa from a makeshift shop owned by a lame labourer, who had set it up right behind the mill, and they ran back home, shouting and screaming in joy.

When he was passing the district courts on his way to the bus stand, he saw the procession lurching towards the court. He, too, began to walk behind it. As he came closer to the procession, a policeman, who was standing by the roadside, shouted to him, asking him to stop. When he tried to turn towards the bus stand, another policeman sent him back. Turning back, he went and joined a group of people, standing outside a shop, built on a raised platform.

'All around the district courts, within the periphery of one kilometre, all processions and gatherings have been banned until the third of next month. That is why we appeal to the members of the rickshaw and tonga unions that they must not go beyond the chowk. They should end the procession here and disperse. If they fail to do so, the entire responsibility for violating the law and order shall rest on their shoulders.'

These words were being blared out by a loudspeaker fixed atop a jeep parked near the district courts. But as the procession of rickshaw pullers wended its way towards the courts, they began to shout slogans even more lustily. Their sloganeering and the blaring announcements were threatening to devolve into pandemonium. The rickshaw pullers leading the procession had now reached the iron gates of the district courts. The man wearing a pair of thick glasses, sitting in a rickshaw on the left, was now standing up, punching his fist into the air, and shouting slogans in his throaty voice, at the top of his bent.

Suddenly, the gates of the district courts clanged shut. Some policemen, armed with lathis, who were standing in front of the gate decided to stop the procession from moving forward. At the back, the rickshaw pullers suddenly massed into a big crowd. In front of the gates, the rickshaws had piled up just the way ants start swarming over the ground in the rainy season once they slither out of an anthill. One could see a sea of rickshaws surging forward. Now the men had got off their vehicles and untying the flags from the handlebars started waving them, shouting slogans with renewed gusto. Holding the flags in one hand, and dragging their rickshaws with the other, they had now pulled up right outside the gate. The tongas coming up behind had split into two groups, with one half moving towards one side of the road and the other half moving towards the other side. These tongas, too, were now slowly inching towards the gate.

'Go back, or there will be a lathi charge.'

As soon as this fresh statement was heard, suddenly countless policemen materialized on the scene, as if from nowhere. They hit out blindly, their lathis landing on everyone around. Some of them came charging towards the tonga wallahs, who were standing a little way off. Every horse received two blows. The moment they heard the sounds of the raining blows and the screeching of the wheels, the horses simply took off in different directions. All this commotion made it seem as though the earth was convulsing. An emaciated horse, pulling one of the tongas, collapsed in a heap, right outside that shop, where bahoo's brother was standing. Shocked, and flying over the horse's neck, the tonga wallah came crashing down a few metres away, near the road's edge. Hamstrung by the frame, still half-bent and kneeling, a hind leg of the horse was crushed under the tonga's wheel, and its saddle fell to the right side of the frame. Exactly at that moment, a ferocious-looking policeman who was running alongside, landed a sharp blow on the horse's back. As if this too had not satisfied him, he turned towards the tonga wallah, and hurling abuses, brought his lathi down heavily on the man's shins.

The people who stood watching on the raised platform outside the shop were so scared that they immediately ran away. But in a spontaneous gesture, bahoo's brother ran towards the tonga wallah, and raising him to his feet, said, 'Bhai, are you hurt very badly?'

The tonga wallah first gave him a very strange look, appraising him, and then cast an indifferent gaze at the horse, and said, 'Even if I'm badly hurt, what can you do? Can you fetch sanjeevani booti and make me drink it?'

This twisted response left bahoo's brother perplexed, but unmindful of his presence, the tonga wallah began to saddle the horse again, securely. His turban lay in the middle of the road, and his dishevelled, unwashed, grimy hair was now spattered with dust. As his wrap-around, with its patterned design, fell open, his emaciated legs stared out of his grimy underwear, somewhat strangely. His trimmed beard and moustache on his dark, rugged and taut face looked as if they had been painted on.

Bahoo's brother found him extremely repulsive. For a while, standing aside, he stared at him. While adjusting the saddle, the tonga wallah cracked a whip, and the horse tried in vain to get on to its feet. It wasn't clear whether he was muttering expletives to the horse or to someone else, but the moment the tonga wallah cracked his whip again, the horse was instantly back on its feet. Then muttering in the same vein, he continued to adjust the saddle. It was as though he had forgotten all about his wrap-around and his turban.

The fall had taken the skin off the horse's forelegs and blood oozed from its right knee. Unmindful of all this, the tonga wallah secured the saddle firmly on the horse's back. When he turned to retrieve his turban and his wrap-around, he looked at bahoo's brother who was still standing there, and said, 'Don't bother, oye brother of mine! Every day, we have to go through this. What can a harried man give you, except offensive words? You seem to be a wise man. If lathis are all we get, day in and day out, how do you expect us to do the paath of Shabad Hazaara?'

Talking to himself in this vein, he first secured the wrap-around on his waist, then loosely tied his turban, examined the wheels of his tonga from every corner, and then started spouting expletives at someone, whose name was difficult to understand. Bahoo's brother couldn't make up his mind as to what kind of tonga wallah he was. Until now, he was completely oblivious of the fact that Melu could be among those protesting rickshaw wallahs, and that he, too, could have been beaten up in this merciless manner, resulting in some unexpected tragedy.

The moment this thought hit him, he felt a strange dread run through him. When he looked ahead, he saw a bizarre spectacle before his eyes... All the rickshaws, scattered all around, were lying upside down in a heap. Three or four tongas were also turned on their heads. On the other side of the iron gates, all he could see were policemen milling about. The rickshaw and tonga wallahs, stuffed into two police trucks, were still shouting slogans. Though he looked very hard, he couldn't spot Melu among them. Somewhat confused, he walked across to the same tonga wallah he had just left, who was busy rubbing his knees, and asked, 'Why, Bhai Singha, you'd know whether Melu Singh was also in this procession?'

'Oye, brother of mine, I haven't cracked Melu's knuckles that I should know. There are twenty such Melus going about, feeling exasperated.' The tonga wallah, once again, spoke in the same coarse manner. Then tightening the surcingle over the horse, he asked, 'If I'm not wrong, are you asking about that Melu who lives in the basti opposite the mill?'

'Hanh, hanh, he is my brother-in-law. My elder sister is married to him.'

'Why couldn't you find someone else? Did you go all the twelve miles with a lantern to look for someone like him?' Unmindful of the charged atmosphere all around, the tonga wallah spoke with dripping sarcasm, 'It'd have been much better had you pushed your sister into a well.' When bahoo's brother maintained a studied silence, refusing to respond to him, the tonga wallah changed his tune. Lowering his voice, he said, 'Don't be angry with me, oye brother of mine! God has given us such twisted tongues. What can we do? Why talk of your brother-in-law alone? Everyone is like that. All of them take drugs, even opium. They give themselves injections, too. Let them be. Except a good deed, they do everything they shouldn't. Your Melu is not so pious that he won't follow the footsteps of these elephantine monsters... It's not that he is to be blamed in any way... It's vagabonds like me who have given him false notions about himself... I told him several times over, Bhai, if you want to save yourself, then go back to your village. Why are you wasting away, here? Life in these towns is like a well. If you don't try and find out about a man buried underneath, he won't even stink. Weh, both the worlds have abandoned us, we have no past, and no future. We are like the lame tail of the camel. What can any bloody fool take away from us? Beyond this, there is no other pit into which we may fall. Our people always looked down upon this profession of tonga driving. But this is what we are condemned to do, now. You are a wise man,

Bhai Singha; it's such a useless profession that it can easily make an addict out of you. Otherwise, why would anyone waste his hard-earned money on dissolving his bones? Moreover, if we weren't hooked to one kind of drug or the other, how would we cope with such a ruthless battering of our limbs? What do we do, bhai, we just can't manage without it. Earlier, mothers used to feed their newborn babies whenever they cried, but now they switch over to the bottle in the second month itself. If a child wails a little too much, they give him a spoonful of "medicine". Now, this new "mother" of ours, the sarkaar, has nothing to offer except lathis. Haven't you seen for yourself? Unless we unite, there is really nothing for us...and if we unite and make a noise, you have already seen what can happen... So tell me, whose "mother" do we address as our "our massi"?'

Talking interminably in this vein, and oblivious to the presence of bahoo's brother, he grasped the reins of the horse and started off towards the district courts. Who knows how his 'gossip' had affected bahoo's brother causing him to forget the commotion he had witnessed close up. Melu was quite far from his mind.

'Oye, why are you standing here, looking so lost? Do you also want to be thrashed like them?' Waving his lathi, a policeman came charging towards him.

Looking somewhat angrily towards the policeman, he, too, turned in the same direction in which the tonga wallah had proceeded earlier.

When he reached the bus stand, he discovered that the people gathered there were also discussing the procession. Holding his counsel, he kept turning back to look over his shoulder, and finally went off towards the mill-basti. On seeing him returning, with a long face, when bahoo asked, 'Bira, what is the matter?' he replied anxiously, 'Nothing really, sister. I think the police have taken Melu and his companions into custody.'

'Police has arrested them? From the procession?'

'Aho. I thought why not find out how he is? I didn't feel like going, leaving you alone in this state.'

Even after hearing a description of what had happened, Melu's bahoo hadn't become as anxious as her brother. Suddenly, as he was reminded of what the tonga wallah had told him, he asked, 'Do they take out these processions as a routine?'

'I don't know. Every day, it's the same thing. Ever since these engine-driven autos arrived, they've started making more noise. It never used to be so bad before.'

'Why?'

'They say if the number of autos goes up, no one will ride the rickshaws. They make five–six passengers sit, not just two, and carry their luggage as well. That way, even if you pay a little more, most people think, it's less.'

Bahoo's brother was listening to all this very intently, as though he were listening to the stories of hell and heaven. He could not really understand how people could think of launching an agitation, or be beaten or hauled up by the police over such a minor matter. He reacted spontaneously, 'Why don't they stop these engine autos, if they are cutting into other people's livelihood?'

'You're really naive. Why would anyone bother? The officers are there to give licences and collect the taxes. Why would they care about what you drive, be it an auto or an aeroplane?'

'But then this is really too much. At this rate, everyone will be squabbling with everyone else.'

'Do you think it's not happening already? Every day, it's

the same sad story.'

'What if Melu were to buy a rickshaw with an engine? Wouldn't that be much better?'

'It costs eight–ten thousand rupees. You talk as if it's just a question of buying a rattle!'

'Eight...ten...thou...sand?'

For bahoo's brother, all these things were rather strange. Then suddenly without warning, he asked, 'All right, tell me, do you want me to fetch anything from the bazaar?'

For a while, Melu's bahoo fell silent. Then she spoke in a weak voice, 'Well, everything has to be bought. There's nothing at home. There was about a kilo of flour, but that had weevil in it. But let him come back, he'll bring it himself. Why would you, unnecessarily...?'

'He won't come back so early. Who knows when they will be released.'

'You think, they are going to ask them to plough the land there? They'll be released in another two hours or so.'

Bahoo's brother hadn't quite understood anything of the matter at all. But rising to his feet, he said, 'We'll see when he comes. You tell me, what all do you need? We can't just keep waiting for him and let the children go hungry.'

Untying the corner of her chunni, she took out a five-rupee note and handed it over to him and said, 'All right then, take this. Get two kilos of flour. And with the rest, you may get 250 grams of daal, a packet of salt, and some besan.'

But looking at her five-rupee note, bahoo's brother simply said, 'You keep this with you. I've got money.'

Despite all her efforts to stop him, he left. Melu's elder son also went with him. Holding his finger, he said, 'Mamaji, I'll tell you where to buy this stuff from.'

'Why, do you get a discount from this shop?'

'We buy all our stuff from that shop, next to the petrol pump.'

'You don't buy it from any other shop?'

'Hanh, he gives us on credit, which others don't.'

Thus talking to each other, the moment they turned the next corner and hit the road leading to the school, they saw a rickshaw puller go by, his face and head wrapped in a blanket. Releasing his mamaji's finger, the boy ran after him, shouting, 'Oye, papa, oye!'

The rickshaw puller glanced over his shoulder, and then speeding up his rickshaw, turned towards the hospital. Bahoo's brother also suspected that it was Melu. As his face and head were completely covered, like a honey harvester, it was difficult to recognize him. Calling out to the boy, he said, 'Oye, it must be someone else. How could he have come back so soon?'

'No, it's him only. Just look, he's gone towards the hospital.'

'All right, if it's him, then he'll be back in a while. He won't go away to Africa.'

By the time they reached the school, and turned onto the road leading to the petrol pump, Melu had already negotiated the street corner and arrived at the hospital, but before that he cast a hasty look over his shoulder. Parking his rickshaw next to the wall, and constantly looking back as if he was a thief, he walked through the verandah of the general ward, and headed for the operation theatre. Going past Dheesa, who was sitting on the stool outside the room, he first signalled to him, and then walked out to wait for him outside. From there, he couldn't see the outer road.

'What's the matter? Why have you covered your face and head like this? Have you fought with someone?' asked Dheesa, baring his toothless gums from behind his thick lips, and then munching the groundnuts he always carried in the pockets of his black trousers, he turned around and went towards the operation theatre.

Without any hesitation, he opened the door of the operation theatre and took Melu inside. After dipping cotton in lukewarm water, he cleaned the blood out of his hair, and then snipped off the bits that stuck close to his ears. After cleaning up a big, gaping wound, he said, 'It looks as if you have been hit by a lathi. What happened? Did you actually come to blows with someone?'

Wincing, Melu said, 'Why would I, yaar? In front of the district courts, a heifer suddenly came in front of me and I lost control. There was a wall, towards the left. I took a toss and crashed into it. It was the edge of the platform near the wall that hurt me.'

'Melu Singha, why do you try and pull a fast one on us? It's a routine affair for us.' Dipping a piece of bandage into a red-coloured medicine and wrapping it over his wound, Dheesa said, 'Oye, brother of mine, if you think that I'm only as good as an animal, then it's all right.'

Embarrassed, Melu started swearing in the name of all kinds of things. Tightening the bandage around his head, Dheesa said, 'Doesn't matter. Don't tell me if you don't want to. Even if you were to, what would we get in the bargain, daal? We go for a friend's friendship, not his bad habits!'

It was mainly to escape his insistent questioning that Melu decided to tie his blood-soaked turban over his head in a hurry. Then glancing towards the machines, scissors, stethoscopes and several other equally strange objects inside the operation theatre, he asked, 'Are you allowed to tie a bandage in this room?'

'Did you come for the bandage because some sahab told you to?' Dheesa first picked up the blood-soaked cotton and bandages, threw them all into a dustbin, washed his hands and then said, 'Bhai Singha, it's our writ that runs large here. Till four o'clock, no one even dares enter this place. Do you understand?'

From day one, Dheesa had been so, both candid and carefree. In school, too, he had been the most mischievous of them all. Who knows what game he played, but he had joined as a chowkidar in this hospital. Slowly, he had worked his way up, and now, it was difficult to say what 'position' he occupied. But his writ actually ran in the entire hospital. He would make expensive medicines available to his friends, free of charge. If needed, he would put in a word with the doctor to examine his friends out of turn. He had become a 'fixer'. He had been working in this very hospital for the past twelve or thirteen years. Who knows what kind of foxy tricks he deployed, but he would easily manage to make a good deal of extra money over and above his salary. When it came to gambling, he wouldn't let anyone else win. In the basti on the outskirts, he had bought a four-marla plot, and constructed a kotha, too. But he lived in the quarters allocated by the hospital. Though one wouldn't even give him a second look, he had married a second time. His first wife had either been poisoned or had died of some disease. He had two sons from his first wife, and a daughter from the second one. He would always flaunt his 'position' and talk in a rather officious manner.

'Dheesiya, come, why don't we go to the village together?' Melu suggested casually, for lack of anything better to say.

Wiping his hands on a white towel, he said, 'Why would

we go to the village now? Do we have to lick the leftovers of the jats, there? Here, everyone comes and touches my feet. There, no one ever spoke to me without hurling an abuse first. And if at this stage I decide to go back and become dependent on them once again, who would call me wise? Besides, what is left there now that I could call my own? My parents have passed away. There is a kothri, which my younger brother has grabbed. Do you expect me to set up a cold storage in the village and then look after it?'

Without a word, Melu walked out. Turning back, he asked, 'Do you want me to take any tablets?'

Pulling three–four golden strips out of the deep, bulging pockets of his white coat, and handing them over to him, he said, 'You take one before you go to bed. If the pain is unbearable, then take another one. I'll do the bandage again tomorrow, around this time.'

Walking through the verandah of the general ward, Melu was thinking to himself, 'What kind of karmas had Dheesa done in his previous life that having been born in the same vehra as he, having studied up to class four in the same school as he, and having winnowed in the fields in the same way as he himself, Dheesa was now almost the owner of this hospital, but he, Melu, was no more than a rickshaw puller.' (It was as though, in the last seven years, he had begun to hate this expression. On so many occasions he had thought of giving up this work, and starting something else. He had tried too, but it had not worked. He wanted to part with the body, but now this body would not let him be; and with each passing day, its burden was becoming more and more oppressive.)

The moment Melu stepped out of the hospital, he wrapped the blanket around his face and head, the way he had done earlier, and started pushing his rickshaw. Rather than turn towards the school, he hit another road, the one that ran in front of the mill. From there, going past the railway crossing, he went towards the official quarters of the railway employees, located in the west. Peddling his rickshaw on the road next to the canal, he felt as though his legs were giving way. Stopping under the shade of a tahli, he took a tablet out of a small, plastic box and started chewing it. Replacing the box in his pocket, he looked about, but did not spot even a single person for miles on end. In order to tie his turban again, when he took the chaddar off his head and looked at his emaciated legs, he felt as though they belonged to someone else.

'This body seems to be giving up. At this rate, how much longer will it work?' he spoke aloud, as if he was searching for answers within. That moment, when he saw a jeep approaching from the direction of the canal, he simply stood there, with his back towards the road.

Once the jeep had trundled past, Melu gently felt the bandage on his head, and covered it with a few, loose folds of his turban. After chewing the tablet, and swallowing it, he turned the rickshaw in the direction of the canal.

On reaching the bank of the canal, he discovered that a stretch, which almost seven years ago was no more than a kuccha, pebbled track, was now a road that ran its serpentine course through a thousand-year-old fortress, and went circling the monstrous chimneys of the thermal plant, before merging finally with the Grand Trunk Road. Towards its right, starting from the canal and continuing down to the Grand Trunk Road, there was a huge parapet, more than the height of a man, made of wire mesh and iron poles. Towards the right side of this parapet, one could see a long stretch of thermal-plant buildings, residential quarters, and a strange-looking barbed-wire fence that blocked entry into that area; all in all, an entire new town appeared to have sprung up there. It was his first close look at this new town. As his gaze ran from below up to the large chimneys that looked somewhat like oversized buckets turned upside down, he trembled and got off his rickshaw, feeling as though the rickshaw was going to tumble into the canal.

Somewhat restless, he started peering up at the chimneys once again. On top of the chimney facing him, he could see some eight–ten persons hanging, looking like small bers. Suddenly, he felt as though those persons were beginning to fall off. Blinking over and over again, he kept gazing at them, stunned. Owing to the fading light of the setting sun, the shapes of those persons were not clearly visible. But after a while, they became more well defined. Strapped to iron ropes, and lowered from the top of the chimney with pulleys, these persons were standing on swinging logs, holding on to the ropes with one hand, and cleaning the outer surface of the chimney with the other. The upper portion of the chimney was now shinning and appeared much brighter compared to the portion beneath the swinging logs, which still appeared smudged and grimy with long, irregular lines caused by constant exposure to rain.

'What if someone were to fall from that height…?' This time, again, the words just escaped his lips, involuntarily.

That moment, again, he felt his legs trembling. Leaving his rickshaw by the roadside, he went and sat on the grass, along the bank of the canal, though his eyes were still fixed on those persons who were walking freely on the swinging logs, from one end to the other. Suddenly he thought of the day, Kalu, the chowkidar, had advised him to join this thermal plant, saying, 'It's a good job; much better than breaking your legs with constant rickshaw pedalling. Go ahead and join it.'

When he heard the sound of a car honking from behind, he immediately stood up. On the road next to the canal, a green car was speeding along, whipping up clouds of dust. He immediately pulled the rickshaw towards the canal. Whizzing past, and flinging up pebbles in its path, the car went westwards, where the canal rest house stood.

For a while, Melu just stood there, motionless, and then a thought flashed across his mind, as to why he had come there in the first place. That very moment, he turned back and started peddling his rickshaw towards the road. Suddenly he was reminded of how his son had called out to him near the petrol pump, and he felt as though he had come towards this side, only to escape the tyranny of that sound. Even now, he could sense that sound chasing him, almost like a steady shadow.

Pedalling the rickshaw somewhat rapidly, when he came back to the same tahli, under which he had taken that tablet, and started gazing towards the kotha that stood close to a banana grove, he suddenly remembered why he had come over to this side. Turning the rickshaw towards the banana grove, he stopped it near a mulberry bush, and then after opening the latch of a ramshackle gate, walked right in. On hearing his footfalls, a dog as big as a bear barked from inside, and at that very moment, Shilte's harsh voice was heard, 'Who is it, oye?'

'I, Melu,' he called, stopping a few yards away from the kothri.

After pacifying the dog, Shilta called out to him, 'Come on in; come on in.'

When he reached the front door of the kothri, Shilta was sitting on a cane stool outside, smoking his hookah. Scratching his topknot with one hand, and blowing out smoke through his nostrils, he spoke in Baghri, 'You come any time you want to. Right now, I don't have that "thing" for you. Come tomorrow, early morning.'

Squatting near Shilta's makeshift chulha, Melu said, 'Oye, you big contractor, first ask at least, why I've come here. You just start shooting your mouth off, without any prelude... You'll remain what you are...a dumb fool.'

After dragging on the hookah deeply, as Shilta pulled the pipe away from his thick moustaches, it was as though the wrinkles on his wizened face had burst into a sudden, spontaneous smile. First, he placed his rugged hand, with crumpled, thick fingers, on his head, and then slowly dragging it over his broad, furrowed forehead, narrow eyes, bulbous nose and scraggly beard, he brought it down to his chin, and then scratching it, again spoke in Baghri, 'I'm still as innocent as a suckling child, who doesn't even know whether the likes of you come here to dig earth or just make rounds of this place to feed their addiction, for their own father's sake?'

'Oye bapu, I mainly came to ask you, bhai, whether or not Dulla had come here?' It was as if Melu had conceded his defeat to Shilta.

'Let the darkness descend, then all these Dulla-Shullas shall come cowering like owls into this dark kothri.'

'Who can possibly argue with you like a dog, and waste his breath?' Melu said, as he got up to move towards the so-called 'palace' of Shilta, right behind the garden, 'I'm going to lie down for a while. If someone comes, do tell him that I'm here. Is it alright?'

Shilta went back to smoking his hookah. He crossed the field where radish had been planted, and had barely reached the mango tree, when Shilta the gardener hollered out, 'Oye, you… Put away "this father of yours" somewhere.'

Melu remembered that he had left his rickshaw outside near the mulberry bush. Turning back, he dragged the rickshaw inside the gate and parked it in the shade of the kothri, and again, proceeding towards the manji outside the kothri behind the garden, he lay down upon it.

Still, the day had not quite spent itself. And no one was expected to come here before sunset. Lying face up on that loosely strung manji, he began to feel somewhat restless. Turning over to his side, when he looked ahead, he saw that close to the bed of cauliflowers, two male sparrows were squabbling, as if they wanted to swallow each other alive. Sometimes, one would be on the top, and sometimes, the other. The one on top would drive the other one crazy by digging its beak repeatedly into its flesh. For a long time, he stared at them. Then another one came and swooped down so suddenly upon the male sparrow on top, that the squabbling duo abandoned their fight and flew off and perched themselves on the branches of the tree right opposite. Rather than follow them, the third sparrow flew towards the road, crying 'cheen…cheen…' with such a flourish as though it had already conquered the fort of Chittaurh.

Watching this little scene had calmed Melu's agitated mind, somewhat. For a long time, lying ramrod straight on his back, he stared at that tree with the sparrows on it. Once or twice, he tried to make sense of it but couldn't, as he found it difficult to fathom what kind of land they were fighting over. And also why another sparrow had to intervene to settle their dispute or why she couldn't let those idiots just kill each other. Battle-weary, they would probably give up on each other.

Shilta hollered once again. When he looked in the direction

of the kothri, he saw both Dheeru and Dulla walking towards him. Dheeru was sporting a polka-dotted turban and a dark blue wrap-around. Dulla was wearing the same old clothes, a khaki coat with torn pockets, and an oversized, crumpled pyjama, and on his feet were an old pair of juttis, stitched and repaired, many times. As Dulla approached him, he laughed out loud, baring his teeth blackened with overuse of tobacco, 'So, you're enjoying a good sleep, you leader of the gang. Scared of the lathi blows, look where he has chosen to hide himself, in the Red Fort of Delhi.'

Tying up the loose end of his turban and smiling through his hollow cheeks and sunken eyes, Dheeru said, 'It looks as if he has won many "medals" today, no less than five or seven.'

'So, vile one, how are things with you?' Seeing him flat on the manji, Dulla came closer, shook him by his shoulder, burst into a guffaw and said, 'You're lying as if your mother is already dead. Oye, what is the matter, henh?'

When Melu was about to turn over on his side, the loose end of his turban came undone. Seeing the bandage on his head, Dheeru spoke with some concern, 'Oye, he is actually carrying a certificate of his "leadership". Where were you at that time, bhai?'

Melu wasn't keen on responding to any of their questions. Settling down on the manji next to him and thumping his back, Dheeru said, 'Doesn't matter. The lions have to face all this. This is nothing. You have a long way to go. Bhai sahab, this is just the beginning of a long journey... Long journey, but eyes squinted; Shilta the gardener is on your side, so why should you worry?'

Melu was in no mood to appreciate such juvenile talk. Trying to force him off the manji by humouring him like a small child, Dulla laughed and said, 'Come on, get up now. Let's play a game of cards.'

'You play if you want to. I'm not interested,' said an exasperated Melu.

'That's all. As they say, "she is looking for Baba's shoulder after walking barely half a mile". You're really made for big things, man. You'll go a long way.' Dulla got up from the manji, making a face as though he had tasted something bitter.

Letting Melu be, both of them went and sat down upon a pile of sacks lying outside the shack. Pulling out a pack from his pocket, Dheeru started shuffling the cards. Dulla sat down upon a mud-soaked sack, without even dusting it. They threw a small, tattered piece of durrie in front of them. When Dheeru was dealing the cards, seeing a forlorn look in Melu's eyes, Dulla laughed and said, 'You know, friend, his story is quite similar to that of Kamli, in whose case, it doesn't matter whether or not she goes to her in-laws' house… Once, someone like Melu went to Dilli. When he returned after twelve years, someone asked, "So tell us, brother, what all did you see in Dilli?" And the brother says, "Well, nothing really." The questioner was surprised and asked, "Oye, you saw nothing? Then, where were you, all this while? In a dark pit?" And the fellow retorts, "I simply used to practise this trick of doing 'labour without rewards' there".'

On hearing Dulla's words, Dheeru also started laughing loudly. Holding his cards close to his chest, he said, 'Bhai Melu Singha, you are not fit to live here. It'd have been much better for you to have gone back to the village. There, you may still be able to do something. But what will a straight and simple man like you do in such a town? No one gives a dime if you ask for it. And they will take less than a minute to auction off a fellow like you, right there, at the crossroads.'

Lying quietly, Melu was gazing at two–three leaves, hanging precariously from a nearly withered branch of the mango tree. His companions were so completely lost in their game of cards that they seemed to have become oblivious of his physical injury, even his existence.

Carrying a hookah and walking in his peculiar flip-flop manner, almost like a plough heaving up and down, Shilta came and stood by Melu's head. Rising, Melu sat up on the manji. First, Shilta kept staring towards Dulla and Dheeru, but when Melu was about to tie his turban, looking at his bandage, Shilta spoke in Baghri, 'Bhai Melu, you seem to have injured yourself badly. You must apply a paste of turmeric mixed with mustard oil on it. It'll heal very soon.'

Melu paid him no attention, whatsoever. Appraising Shilta's tough, supple body, his dumb-bell like, ebony-black calf muscles and his grimy dhoti, pulled up from behind his knees, his thoughts drifted away, and a smile appeared on his face. 'Now, look at this. Here, Shilta is also behaving like Lukmaan, the legendary vaid,' Dheeru said in jest, looking at Shilta furtively.

But Shilta turned solemn as he ran his hand over his topknot, flared his nostrils and rolled his eyes, no bigger than a ber seed, and spoke in Baghri, 'Oye, who do you think I am? I've worked for an Angrez for ten long years. Unlike you, that Angrez was not a rustic lout. The lieutenant I served used to get something like four thousand rupees as his salary. He was a tall, strapping man, as young as a ghost and absolutely gora-chitta.'

Dulla laughed heartily. 'Unless the old woman dies, the plough will not turn askew'. Oye stupid fool, what are you trying to say?'

'What am I trying to say?' In a bid to shake the mud off his foot, Shilta thumped it on the ground, and then quickly thrusting the pipe into his mouth to drag on his hookah, he released the smoke and spoke in Baghri, 'What do you animals know who the Angrez really were? During their Raj, both the goat and the lion used to drink water at the same ghaat. Now, do these buggers even bother about anyone?... This ox of ours goes around singing and dancing even if someone gives him a five-paisa coin by mistake. When the Angrez were here, I'd give away as much as five rupees as baksheesh to others. Do you have any idea when the frogs actually drink water? You're just barking your head off unnecessarily.'

The hybrid language Shilta often used made it extremely difficult for them to comprehend what he meant. His speech was never very coherent. That's why most of them would simply laugh at his expense and let things be. But he was so stubborn that he would often argue with them, even when no one had asked him to intervene. On his own he would start talking about his wife, whom he had visited in his village no more than five or six times in the past five years. They had been married for thirty years, but Shilta had never stayed with her for more than two months; though they had seven children. The elder daughter had been married off, and two of his younger sons assisted his brother in farming, as they still retained some of their ancestral land.

'Oye, you crazy fool, you just talk without any rhyme or reason. Sometimes you start abusing our "ox". Why can't you go and settle in your own village?' Dulla repeated what he had told him on numerous other occasions, too, 'You let your wife live like a widow, and here you are busy kneading dough all the time. Who will call you, the son of an Angrez, a wise man? When you already have four acres of land, why do you have to go through this ox-like grind of digging up grass?'

In a bid to revive the flame, Shilta repeatedly pulled on the pipe and tried stoking the dying embers by blowing over them. A secret he had kept from all of them was that all his three brothers had failed to redeem the five or six acres of land his father had mortgaged long before his death. And now in order to marry off their children, they were planning to sell that land at a much lower rate.

Looking at Shilta's dark, rugged face, Melu felt as though his wrinkles had sagged, all of a sudden. Then suddenly Shilta changed his tune and spoke in a rather harsh voice,'All right, first you tell me, should I get the "masala" right away or a little later?'

'We'll take it from you before we go. It's still daylight.' After Dulla announced this, they paid Shilta no attention. Kicking the wet mud dykes, rather casually, he went off towards the other side of the garden.

Today, Melu felt as if something in him was collapsing and sinking deep inside. His head injury had begun to trouble him now. Without a word, he lay down on the manji once again.

'Oye Melu! Today, your delicate one was to come.' It was as if Dulla had touched a raw nerve in him. When Melu didn't respond, Dulla became somewhat serious and said, 'Listen to me—just go back to your village. You've been here for seven years now. What have you gained? Of course, you own this rickshaw, now. But you're also wearing out your bones. Aren't you? Bachelors like us just get drunk at sunset and strut around like peacocks, and you keep peddling until midnight. You don't eat or drink anything. If you have managed to buy yourself a rickshaw after all these years of gruelling labour, then cursed be such a way of earning money. You have had to pay a price for it as well. Oye, crazy fellow, half your energy has been drained by your family responsibilities, and the other half by your greed. What is the end result of all this greed? Now you earn five rupees a day, and need snuff worth at least four rupees to get through the day. How long can your woman manage with the single rupee you manage to save? You never know, some day, some bachelor might find her in that state, and run away with her. Then you'll have to go around, drumming up support in your favour.'

Dheeru's laughter rang through the air. Melu felt that both of them were bent on humiliating him. Lying ramrod straight, he kept staring at the tahli leaves that were about to fall off the tree, and yet they didn't. It was as if they couldn't bear to be separated from the tree.

Slowly, the sun melted. Dulla and Dheeru were busy playing cards. Dheeru was losing to Dulla. Riding the crest of victory, Dulla was on top of the world. When it had become really dark, all of them got up to leave. Handing over a five-rupee note to Dulla, Dheeru said, 'Take this. You take another two rupees from me tomorrow. But make sure, this corpse has his drink before you take him back.'

When both of them fell about laughing, again, Melu felt as though they were digging him out of his grave. Catching hold of him by his arm, Dulla spoke to him critically, 'Why don't you get up, oye, my house of poverty! Had you been beaten as much as we were, your wife would have certainly gone back to her parents and wailed her heart out. Come on, let's go. Let's arrange to eat a morsel or two.'

Slipping into his juttis, Melu decided to accompany them, as though he had no control over his own reflexes. After buying half a peg of country liquor from a nearby shanty, Dulla paid him three rupees, and they came out on the road, each pedalling his own rickshaw. Turning his vehicle towards the canal, Dulla said, 'Come on, today, we'll drink by the bank of the canal... Sometimes, we should also kick up life, the way these affluent youngsters do.'

Dheeru turned his rickshaw in the same direction. As Melu couldn't think of anything much, he too started following them.

As they hit the track leading to the canal, they found that the place was flooded with light. Melu had never seen so many power-house lights mingling with the street lamps and the green and red lights on top of the chimneys. Getting off the rickshaw, he started walking behind them, ever so slowly, staring at the glow-worms suspended right in the middle of this floodlight. And suddenly, the glow-worms rose so far above him that they almost began to touch the skies. Since the lights had suffused the ground, their faces appeared to be dark, and the shapes, too, looked much more ominous than they would by day. Suddenly, Melu's eyes fell upon the patch of glow-worms to his left, above which he could spot men walking around on a wooden platform, and a sudden cold sigh escaped his lips, as though he was going to fall off the very same platform.

'Come on, boys!' Stopping his rickshaw as soon as he got on to the track, Dulla pulled out two glasses from the hollow under the seat, and went to sit on the grass by the side of the canal. Opening the bottle, and holding it up to the light, he poured small amounts of the liquor into their glasses, and then summoning Dheeru, said, 'Come on, bhai, you first. Today, you're the winner.'

'No!' Lifting his face, his hands resting upon his back, and then settling down in a somewhat awkward posture, Dheeru replied, 'First you pull your bhai out of his troubles. He really seems to be down today.'

'You're absolutely right,' said Dulla, looking at Melu, who stood there, with his hand upon his handlebar. 'What kind of trouble is he in? Oye, come along, you, the perpetual worrier! Drink it and you'll turn into an unstoppable parrot, right away.'

Stepping forward as Melu saw Dulla hold up the glass in his hand, Melu felt as if he was actually tempted. But coming closer and sitting down next to them, he said, 'Na bhai, I don't feel like drinking today.'

'Oye, you brother-in-law of mine, are you on a fast because it happens to be a Tuesday or something?' Dheeru spoke somewhat peevishly.

Then both of them tried very hard to persuade Melu, but he simply refused to relent. Guzzling down the contents of his glass in a single go, and filling it with water, Dulla said, 'Bhai, it seems today Melu Singha is riding a high horse. Tell us, what's the matter, really?'

'There is nothing much.' Melu's voice was low, 'I just don't feel like it.'

'He'll not tell you; I'll tell you what the matter is.' Emptying his glass in a single swallow, Dheeru said, 'Today, he is hurt because of what we said. Otherwise, there is nothing. You just ask him.'

'All right, you declare on an oath!' Dulla looked at Melu, as he spoke, 'If this is the reason, brother, then please forgive us. You know, it's in our nature to talk nonsense.'

'No, no...there is nothing like that.' With these words, Melu lay down on the grass.

Dulla and Dheeru fell silent. After a while, tapping his shoulder, Dulla spoke in a somewhat tipsy, though solemn voice, 'Do you think, bhai, we are just making up all these stories?'

Then without so much as waiting for Melu's response, he started off on his own, 'Look, this moonlight is my witness. You may have just one cause for sorrow, but my guts are in shreds. These jats, my patrons, got me to serve a twenty-year term in jail in connection with a murder case. With money power, they managed to get away, clean. It's my responsibility to marry off my three sisters, and all of them are simply waiting to be packed off. And look at their brother; he is not equipped to earn anything. All the chachas and tayyas are sitting around, watching the tamasha. I'm the only breadwinner. And I can't do without these bad habits that are bleaching my bones. If we keep worrying ourselves sick over all this, then we won't even be in a position to send whatever little money we do manage to send home... Now, you decide, how happy I really am! And as for Dheeru, all he has to sport is a colourful turban; otherwise, he is in a far worse condition than I am. It's another matter that he keeps boasting without any reason. Don't you know that his entire family is dependent upon his income?'

Turning around, Melu gave Dulla a look that seemed to say he knew that what he was listening to were nothing but lies. He had never spoken of such things to him ever before. All he knew was that Dulla had come to town much earlier than he had (it had been several years now) and yet he hadn't been able to buy his own rickshaw; he was still plying a rented one. Being from the same caste and community, they were quite close, but it was his first-ever glimpse of this particular facet of Dulla. Not only would he laugh and joke loudly all the time, or in his characteristic nonchalant manner, indulge in gossip, he would also make others laugh at his own expense. He was also quite friendly with other rickshaw pullers and members of their union. Whenever they held a meeting or a procession, he would be spinning around like a spool of thread. How many times had he been beaten to a pulp by the police. Even after five–six days in jail, he would return, laughing as though he were returning from a wedding.

'Don't do this to us, Melu Singha.' Dulla's voice had suddenly turned solemn, 'Have a swig or two. Then I'll tell you what you are, and what I am. And if you refuse to drink, you'll have to swear in the name of my youth!'

And after drinking half its contents, Dulla handed the glass over to Melu. Stretching out, Melu took the glass and emptied it in one swallow. He didn't even drink water, thereafter. With a tingling sensation running down his spine, he looked at Dulla, furtively. Dulla was pouring whatever was left into the two glasses, and handing a glass to Dheeru. Looking at Melu, he spoke in the same tone, 'Now, you listen to me carefully.' Then holding up his glass in front of the lights, he kept staring at him, for some time. After a while, gritting his teeth, he shouted a filthy abuse, and throwing his peg into the canal, he nearly shrieked, 'If I could, I'd set this bloody water on fire. O bloody hell, is there anything special about it?… Oye, the stubborn one, I'm totally drunk, now!'

Speaking incoherently and almost like a man possessed, when he tossed his head, his turban went flying off and landed at Melu's feet. Picking up the turban with trembling hands, Melu looked at Dulla again. His topknot had come undone and his hair lay tumbled around his neck.

'What kind of an accursed existence is this, Melu Singha? We're just like the dogs, dogs really.' Pulling his hair together into a knot, Dulla shrieked in the same loud voice. Melu was terrified. Scared, Dheeru too started staring at his sieve-like face.

'Look, this is what it is.' Taking his turban from Melu and tying it around his head, 'For our kind of people, the only liberation is what comes after death. Till now, we could still earn enough by the evening to be able to feed ourselves. Now ever since these auto-rickshaw drivers have deprived us of our livelihood, no one is ready to give us a pie. We aren't in a position to do any other kind of labour—because of the bad company we are in. Wait and see the way we'll all die. Do you understand what I'm saying?'

And then he stood up again. Removing the seat of his rickshaw, he put the glasses back into the hollow underneath, and without saying another word, he turned the rickshaw towards the station. Without arguing, Dheeru and Melu did the same. As he was pedalling the rickshaw off the raised mound, Melu saw that Dulla was wiping his eyes with a corner of his turban. From the raised mound itself, he had started plying his rickshaw at such speed that the moment he reached 'Kohlu's orchard', his seat went flying through the air. But Dulla didn't look back. Overcome by an unknown fear, Melu and Dheeru too had come speeding down after him.

As they neared the railway track, Melu felt as though his legs were giving way. Rather than turn right towards the bazaar, Dulla and Dheeru turned left, towards the cinema hall. It was a routine matter for all of them to eat at one dhaba, in that very chowk. As he came closer to the chowk, Melu loosened one end of his turban and covered his face with it. Then after thinking it over, he plied the rickshaw right, towards the bazaar.

Taking the outer road, he came towards the fort via a covered street.

Seeing an eye-piercing light at the main gate of the fort, Melu hesitated. The huge gates of the fort were shut. After parking his rickshaw near an electricity pole, when he pulled at the gate's five–six ser heavy knocker, Kalu spoke from inside at that very moment, 'Who is it, bhai?'

'Melu.'

'What do you want here at this hour, to dig earth or something?' Mumbling in protest, Kalu walked towards the door. Pushing open the heavy planks of the wicket gate, he peeped out and said, 'What is it?'

'I'll tell you. First, you let me in.'

'Yaar, you really shouldn't drop in at such an unearthly hour.' Kalu spoke in a peevish tone, throwing open the wicket gate, 'Today, we really gave them all a good drubbing. And if a police officer on duty were to see you enter this place now, won't he beat the daylights out of me?'

Melu couldn't think of what to say. But he felt that Kalu was upset today only because he hadn't had a drop to drink. Even Melu wasn't carrying any on his person. He also realized that if Kalu were to smell liquor on his breath, he would be all the more disturbed. Settling on Kalu's manji, he said, 'I'm going to stay with you tonight.'

'O brother of mine, I can't allow this.' Standing at a distance Kalu said, 'Go and make this arrangement with someone else. I'm a family man, with a wife and children to support. If anything goes wrong, I won't be able to recover from it, all my life.'

'All right then, remember this day.' It was as if Melu complained to Kalu with all the eloquence at his command and then opening the wicket gate, emerged on to the street.

Lost in his own thoughts, Kalu kept staring at him. Then banging the wicket gate shut, he deliberately raised his voice and said, 'Look at him. He behaves as if I'm living off his father's pilshan. You are from the wretched caste of a dog! Once in a while, if you offer me a drink, does it mean, you have bought me over.'

It was as though Melu hadn't heard a word of what he had said. Stepping hard on the pedals of his rickshaw, he approached the station, after crossing the same covered street. While going past the station, he slowed down and that's when a Marwari in a woollen cap, started waving out to him vigorously, shouting at the top of his voice, 'Oye, you, come here, come here.' Then he quickly turned around to go to the platform to pick up his holdall. But by the time he returned, Melu had moved several feet ahead. Muttering under his breath, the Marwari started looking towards the other side of the road. On seeing him get all worked up, Melu felt strangely gratified.

'God bless you, O rickshaw pullers! If you were not to come for another day, we'd probably earn enough to last us for ten days.' Right behind him, Rakha, the coolie, was invoking blessings upon all the rickshaw pullers as he went along his way, slapping his shoulder towel on his red turban. At first Melu felt enraged, but then seeing his rickety legs and his mud-spattered boots, which made a strange splashing sound as he walked, he suddenly felt a surge of sympathy for him. So without reacting to his comment or speaking ill or well of him, he simply went his way.

When he took the same road that he had taken earlier to go to the canal, to return to the cinema hall, he saw a huge crowd outside. But entering the narrow street towards his right, when he reached Chaunda's dhaba, it was completely deserted. Even though it was really very late, he couldn't spot a single soul there. Chaunda's assistant, the cook, was merrily sitting on the platform, next to the tandoor, warming himself.

Shining in the bright, red glow of the fire in the tandoor, his face appeared to be floating, as though disembodied.

Melu parked his rickshaw near the tap, a little away from the slush, and as he came in, asked the cook, 'Oye, cook, what's the matter? There is no one here today. Where is everyone?'

'All of them have simply vanished.' Blowing his nose with one hand, and clicking the fingers of the other, he spoke in Hindi, 'You also make yourself scarce, or you'll be nabbed like a rat in this chilly winter.'

Seeing him rolling his head like a dumroo, and talking in a nonchalant manner, Melu felt enraged. Sitting on the edge of a bench, he asked again, 'Why don't you talk straight? Where have Chaunda and Laloo gone?'

'They have gone to secure your friends' release.' Again, the cook spoke in riddles.

'Which friends?'

'Dulla and Dheeru.'

'Why, what happened to them?' Melu looked at him, surprised.

'Nothing much.' Turning his palms up, the cook spoke lightly, 'They just had a minor scuffle here. There is nothing more to it.'

'Oye, why don't you talk straight, like a man? Why are you shooting your mouth off?'

'You'll be miserable if I tell you the real thing. And if I don't, at least, you'll have your roti in peace.'

Rising to his feet, when Melu positioned himself next to the tandoor and rebuked him in a harsh tone, Maroo became serious and told him how Dulla and Dheeru had picked a fight with an auto-rickshaw driver outside the cinema hall. Things had really come to a head when five–six auto drivers, equipped with lathis, gathered with the intention of beating them up. Snatching a lathi from one of them, Dulla had lashed out at two of them, even broken the windscreen of one of the auto rickshaws. The police arrested Dheeru, Dulla and the two auto drivers. Chaunda had now gone to secure a negotiated settlement for both of them.

Melu asked anxiously, 'So, hasn't Chaunda returned yet?'

'He's been gone for barely five minutes now. Chaunda said, just give roti to whosoever comes and then shoo them off. The policemen are really exasperated with all of you today.' Looking at the plate piled high with dough, Maroo said, 'Now, if you want to have roti, then sit down. Or you just disappear from here. Do you understand what I'm saying?'

This new complication had preoccupied Melu to such an extent that he had almost forgotten about his own roti. Instructing Maroo to make a couple of rotis, and settling down on the bench right opposite, he asked in a somewhat dispirited voice, 'But how did the fight begin?'

Tearing away a ball of dough from the kneaded flour, Maroo rolled it into a chapatti, and making a swishing sound, as he pushed it inside the tandoor, he said, 'Do you think, while picking a fight or while thinning out lassi, people consult the horoscope of Beli Ram, the Brahman? There was some old animosity rattling deep inside. They were dead drunk, and so started abusing each other. Then things just went out of hand. What else?'

It was as though Melu's mind was in a logjam. He felt as if this entire matter had woven a strange web inside his head. Once or twice, he strained his brain to think as to what could possibly be done, but he couldn't think of a solution—it was as though someone had lost his path on a pitch-dark, dust-laden night. After placing rotis in a steel plate, when Maroo called out to him, Melu was so distracted that he paid him no attention.

'O yaar, have you gone deaf?' When Maroo spoke in a somewhat brusque manner, jolting him out of his reverie, Melu picked up the plate and went off.

While eating his roti, he kept staring at the soot-laden tin roof of the dhaba, the piles and piles of sacks and the wooden planks of the windows. The old table, on which he had kept his plate, would shake each time he tore a piece off his roti. His bench was also rickety and shaky. Everything, the utensils on the platform and the big vessels meant for cooking daal or vegetables, an aluminium basin, a bowl for grinding chutney, and the three–four-year-old calendars hanging on the yellowing wall behind Maroo's back, appeared to have been smoked out. Everything seemed strange and dreadful to him. With each passing moment, he was getting more and more restless.

Maroo was still talking incessantly. Each time he slapped the roti from one hand to the other, applying unusual force, his hair would fall over his face. The moment he jerked his neck back to throw the locks off his face, his bloodshot eyes would start smouldering, creating waves of fear in Melu's heart. The straggly hair of his moustache and beard, unusually long and ugly nose, thick neck, long ears and cheeks as broad as a palm, all of this made him look somewhat strange. Even today, he was wearing the same old khaki kurta, soaked in grime, its left pocket was torn and hanging low, looking somewhat like the lolling tongue of a dog, and its arms, near the elbow, had big patches sutured on them. Earlier Melu had never paid much attention to his kurta, but today, he kept staring at its tattered collars, and Maroo's bones peeping out of the broken buttons of his kurta near his chest, as though he was setting his eyes upon him for the first time. 'What a grotesque body! What an ugly face!'

'Oye, do you ever have a bath?' While eating his food, Melu suddenly popped this question.

Maroo gave him a strange look, and then baring his broad teeth, he grinned and said, 'Why should I? Do I have to give away cows in charity? To tell you honestly, the first time, it was the midwife who gave me a bath, and now four brothers like you shall bathe me when I go. Bathing twice is more than enough for a man in his entire lifetime. No? Can we lie soaking in water all the time, like buffaloes?' Then after a pause, he spoke solemnly, 'Bhai Singha, you talk big and know how to make stories. I sleep when I want to, and get up when I wish to. You people have a bath and wear clean clothes so that you can attract the attention of women passengers. And when you have nothing much to do, then you take out a procession and frighten people. If you have to get up in the morning at four and light this chulha with wet coals, or face the living hell of having to sit next to it, right up to twelve at night or even beyond, and, on top of that, if you have to constantly suffer the indignities of a man like Chaunda, then I'll ask you if you can ever think of having a bath even in your dreams. Then you'd forget all these things that you're talking about right now, with such gusto. I swear, you'd forget all of this in less than four days.'

Maroo had been working for Chaunda for as many as four years and so Melu had, on many occasions watched Maroo bake rotis, even when he was running a high temperature. Yet strangely he knew virtually nothing either about Maroo or his family. It was the first time ever that he was hearing such things from him, which, though common, were yet so strange. He had always believed—wrongly—that Maroo had a comfortable life. He was becoming a soft pea, as he was feeding himself liberally on meat and masala. But now he wanted to ask him so many questions; about his salary, his wife and children, brothers and sisters, relatives, where his home was, and so on. But he hadn't been able to gather enough courage to ask him even a single question.

After finishing his meal and washing his hands, he asked, 'I'll pay for everything, next month.'

'Next month your "wife" will be back. Then we'll get to see you after six months or so, when she will again go off to her parents' house. And all this while, Chaunda will get after my life. Oye, brother of mine, please pay in a day or two, or he'll deduct it from my salary.'

Melu's pocket was empty. So without a word, he simply left by the back door. Sitting by himself, Maroo continued to mutter something indecipherable, for a long time.

'Oye, I forgot to tell you one thing. Just listen to this carefully before you go,' he shouted to Melu as he was leaving. When Melu came back, he tried to advise him in the manner of a wise old man, saying, 'Now, you'd better go to the police station and make enquiries. Kalu, the constable, is from your village. Just seek his intervention and get this matter involving your friends sorted out. Do it right away. If it drags on too long, it'll only get more complicated. Just like me, Dulla, too, is from a very poor family—what if he loses his head, and they decide to give him a good thrashing! Moreover, these auto wallahs are like scorpions; they go around feeling so important, their foot-long tails up, stiff. They think no end of themselves—so you shouldn't regret it later. The other day, one of them landed up here and spoke in Hindi, "I'll have roasted chicken". Bloody roasted chicken! It's with great difficulty that we get pumpkin here, and he is looking for the roasted legs of a chicken.'

Melu left, once again, without answering. He had barely turned the rickshaw in the opposite direction when the lights went off. He tried very hard to peer through the dark street, but nothing was visible. Guided by his instincts, he kept dragging the rickshaw along the uneven path, close to the wall of the iron foundry, and only when he had turned the corner of the narrow street leading to the cinema hall did he spot some light there. All around, it was still pitch dark. Two or three trucks, and some handcarts and tongas that were parked on the stretch behind the cinema hall had blocked the entire road. He didn't ride the rickshaw, but kept pulling it along.

On reaching the crossroads near the school, he wondered which way to turn. So deep a quandary was it that for a long time, Melu just stood at the crossroads, looking from one side to the other. Suddenly, he felt as though someone had pushed him from behind. Trembling, he turned back, but he couldn't see anyone, as the road was completely deserted. The night was slowly wearing off. He felt the bitter cold was wearing away his ankles. Turning the rickshaw left, he set off in the direction of the street opposite the mill-basti.

As he came closer to his own street, a strange sense of fear overwhelmed him, and he started padding across, almost like a thief stealing his way through. Everything from the broken bricks of the mud-soaked street to the odour of the old houses was the same, and yet everything appeared rather strange to him. In these small, kuccha-yellow houses, looking somewhat like nooks and crannies, lived families of eight or even ten members. Whosoever had entered this street had never been able to leave it. In front of the houses or behind them, towards the right or the left of the street, wherever people found a little space, they had created little 'tenements' out of whatever they could lay their hands on, old bricks, tin sheets or cylinders, jute sacks or the thin planks plucked out of the wooden boxes meant for storing tea or soap. He had never seen a bricklayer or a labourer enter this street; working through the night or day, the men and women had created everything on their own. The narrow corners, in which they otherwise did most of their cooking during the day, were where either a newly wedded couple or two–three children would huddle up and sleep at night. Despite his best efforts, he hadn't been able to leave this sorrowful basti and go elsewhere.

He felt that the light emerging from behind the torn gunny sacks wrapped around the ventilator of a kothri, just ahead of his own, was not only dim but also fearful, just like the expression in Maroo's eyes. When he heard the sound of Prabhu, the old man, coughing inside, he stopped in his tracks. He also felt as though some nuts and bolts of his rickshaw had loosened, and were creating a strange, jarring sound. But when he started walking again, he heard no sound at all.

It suddenly struck him how all the sons and daughters of the old man, Prabhu, had gone off to live in their own houses. Now Mai Dharmo and he were the only ones left. After having served in the mill all his life, he had retired only three years ago. Since that very day, he had been keeping indifferent health. His son, who was working somewhere in Delhi, had come thrice to take him along, but he had refused point-blank. Every time, he would say, 'When all my life I have lived here, why would I go and waste away in a foreign land in my last few years?' It was strange that he didn't feel like stepping out of such a hellhole of a kothri.

The moment this thought of a 'hellhole of a kothri' occurred to him, tremors ran through his body. The next house was his. He slowed to a crawl. Stopping, he appraised the situation. No sound from inside. The tin-pot door frame, which overlooked the verandah and was fitted into a barely three- or four-foot-high outer wall, looked somewhat like Prabhu's lower jaw, as it hung loose, towards one side. Pushing it hard, Melu threw it open; still there was no sign of anyone stirring, indoors. Without making any noise, he brought the rickshaw in, parked it under a roofed-in space near the kitchen, locked it up and yet no sound was heard from inside the kothri.

Melu's heart was beating very fast now. The buzzing sound inside his ears had become louder. His legs seemed to be caving in. First, he kept staring at the dark wooden planks of the doors in front of him, and then he turned away towards the main door. Walking back into the street, he closed the door quietly. As he glanced at the kothri, once again, from its threshold right up to the ledge of the wall, peering hard at several serpentine rows of closely laid bricks, he felt as though some animal was sitting on the edge of the wall. When he looked carefully, he realized that when this wall was being built, some amateur bricklayer had put five or six extra bricks on top of the ledge, something that he had been seeing for the past seven years now. But on earlier occasions, somehow these bricks had never assumed the shape of an animal, the way they had done now.

Tiptoeing, he came right up to the corner of the street. Standing at the corner, when he looked towards the right, he saw no habitation, only large tracts of barren space spread out as far as the eye could see. Walking towards the main road, with his hands buried in his armpits, when he turned around to look in the direction of his basti, once again, a long, deep sigh escaped his lips, involuntarily.

Short of the main road, he stopped near a high mound. This time, when he turned around, he felt as if he was watching a dream. Enveloped in the inky darkness, spread over several miles, and hovering far above the high and low buildings of the town, including the little nooks and crannies they called their home, the old fort appeared like a dark monster from the sky, with its sharp teeth sunk deep into the earth's surface, running amuck, razing to the ground all the bastis that fell in its way, and it was now chasing him, screaming and hollering.

With a cold tremor running through his body, Melu looked towards the road, and he saw a truck trundle past him, screaming, and then turning in, it zipped down to the bus stand. Going past the high mound, he clambered on to the main road. Opening his chaddar, he wrapped it around himself, and then, with hurried steps, proceeded towards the canal.

After having crossed the canal, rather than hit the road leading to his village, he turned towards the old, kuccha pathway. A straight road had now been carved out of that pathway, after the reallocation of land in the area. But the moment he hit that pathway, he felt as though he was still walking under the shade of rows upon rows of bers, keekars, bamboos, jujubes, and several other bushes and thorns growing by its side. Perhaps, this was the reason why his pace had slowed.

Seven years ago, he and his bride had hit this very pathway to come to the town. Bapu had tried his best to dissuade him, saying, 'It isn't going to be easy for you to survive in the town.' But it was his exasperation with being a siri that had made him say, 'If I'm unable to, then I'll return to the village after knocking around for a while... So what's your problem?' In an emotion-choked voice, bapu had told him, 'Oye, simple one, if we can't sense your problem, who will?' But at that point in time, he hadn't really grasped the meaning of his bapu's words.

After coming to the town, he had tried his hand at hundreds of odd jobs, but he had simply refused to return. He had no wish to go back and work as a siri for the likes of Partapa, who would easily go back on their initial promise of giving him food, somewhere in the middle of the season, and start saying things like, 'Now, you'd better bring your roti cooked from home. Who can afford to feed you idlers? Who gives roti these days? Why don't you settle for dry siri? Do your work and collect your wages, for this is the convention now.'

'Oh!' An involuntary sigh escaping him was in recognition of a sudden pain he had experienced. He had hit his foot against a huge stone.

Right ahead was the railway track. After climbing the incline up to the track, he stopped once again. Just like the old fort, the chimneys of the thermal plant seemed to be hovering over the track. It was as though the track had been bathed in a galloping floodlight. But after crossing the railway line, when he looked around at the bristle-filled kuccha pathway, it lay steeped in darkness. Beyond that, far into the distance, the pathway was just as it had been since the days of his grandfathers and great grandfathers. The same briars and brambles, the same old potholes, and the same strange smell of the wild elephant grass, as if everything had been left completely untouched. He felt as if the pathway had been chopped into two parts, and the railway line had been spread out in the middle like a sword, mainly to keep its severed head and its torso at a certain distance from each other...

'But if I return home, what will I say?' Standing upon that

sword-like railway line, and looking towards the dark pathway, when he spoke out aloud, as if to himself, he felt as though his legs, frozen with cold, were beginning to tremble. He sat down upon the track. For a minute, he was so completely dazzled that he lost sense of where he was.

'No.' It was as if his mind had suddenly arrived at a decision, and rising to his feet, he spoke, again to himself, 'It's much better to be home and be hungry than live in this hellhole. If I don't get a siri's job, then I'll work as a daily wager, or eke out a living somehow. What else? We'll see what happens.'

He got up suddenly, and started walking towards the other side of the pathway. Barely a hundred yards down the incline, the pathway appeared to have been lost in the thick, wild overgrowth of the elephant grass. It had completely slipped his mind that ever since the new road had been built, no horse or handcart had crossed along this pathway. As a result, all kinds of wild bushes and briars, including the elephant grass, had mushroomed right in its middle. But he kept pressing on ahead, feeling his way through, somewhat intuitively.

Then out of the dense cover of darkness, he felt as though he had heard the sound of his father coughing, and he stopped. On peering a little harder, he felt that his bapu was actually walking a few steps ahead of him. (On so many occasions in his childhood, Melu had accompanied his bapu to this town, along this very pathway. At that time, he would often hear the sound of his grandfather coughing as he neared these thickets. As this thought struck him, he felt a cold shudder run through his body.) Stopping in the middle of the pathway, he started looking in all possible directions, as if his bapu was somewhere around, fumbling his way through... But the place where, only a couple of hours ago, Melu's bapu had come to leave his bahoo and his children, was miles and miles away from this place where Melu was standing right now. How could he have heard the sound of him coughing from this distance? Melu felt as though he was sinking deeper into the solid earth.

From the other end of this very 'solid' earth, Melu's bapu had, a couple of hours ago, returned to the village, feeling miserable over his separation from his grandsons, then on this very earth, he had heard the lamentations of Dharma's children. On coming closer, when he had peered hard, apart from Dharma's daughter-in-law and his wife, he had also seen a couple of other women—perhaps they were related to them and had come to make anxious enquiries. Or perhaps, they were from the vehra itself, and had come to deliver roti-tuk. But why were the children screaming their lungs out in this wild manner?

That very moment, the track loader surged ahead, thundering like a swarm of locusts, crushing the children's screams under its cacophony, and began to pull down the rest of Dharma's kothri, levelling out the uneven mounds of earth, and then after turning around with the alacrity of a tortoise, it suddenly reversed. Unable to keep looking in that direction anymore, Melu's bapu had simply lowered his eyes, and walked on.

He had walked the entire stretch up to the dharamshala with his eyes lowered, and when on nearing it, he finally raised his eyes, he saw Finnah (the snub-nosed one) step out of their house. He was dressed in a military uniform, and on his turban he had wrapped a red muffler with a floral pattern. Finnah's complexion appeared to be much brighter than before. He greeted Melu's bapu from a distance, 'Chachaji, Sat-Sri-Akal! So tell me, how are you doing? Going strong? I had come mainly to find out about you.'

On coming closer, Melu's bapu thumped his shoulder cheerily, and said, 'You say, how are you? In good health?'

'I'm fine, and with your blessings. Enjoying myself!'

'Are you here on a long leave?'

'Just about a month-and-a-half.'

'I see. You are welcome. Come and sit. Have some "cha-sha" before you go.'

'No, I'll come in the evening. Right now, I have to go and find out about Chacha Dharma. I'm also thinking of going to the town.'

On hearing Dharma's name, Melu's bapu became solemn all over again, and as before, he lowered his head.

When Finnah looked back, somewhat furtively, he sensed that Dyalo was, on one pretext or the other, still looking in his direction. For a while, he thought of staying back, and sitting down for a long gossip session with Melu's bapu, so that he could, at least, give Dyalo a straight look. Within a year, she had grown into a young woman—she appeared much taller than before, too. Her features had shaped well. She had even learnt the art of dressing artfully. But thinking of Dharma Chacha and the tragedy that had struck his family, he said rather abruptly, 'Doesn't matter. Now, I'm here only. We'll keep running into each other, morning-evening. And chacha, if I can be of any service, do let me know. Don't hesitate, henh?'

'Look at him, the crazy one!' Melu's bapu spoke half-admonishing, 'You are not a stranger. Besides, you come after six months or sometimes, even a year. So, it's our duty to look after you, rather than...'

'No, no, chacha! It's always the duty of the youngsters.' Making Melu's bapu glow with a simpering smile, he said, 'All right then, should I go to chacha first? The panchayat might be back much before I land up there.'

With some deep thought overwhelming him, Melu's bapu kept looking after Finnah, as he proceeded towards the dharamshala.

Of all the young men in the vehra, Finnah was the most handsome. He had been in the army now for five years, and his family hadn't felt the lack of anything. Though he was already twenty-four and his family was constantly pressuring him, he was not ready to get married. Whenever they tried to talk to some family for his alliance, he would start lecturing them like an elder, 'Bapu, am I going to grow old so fast? First, let's marry off all the three girls. Then, I'll get fixed up somewhere. There is no famine of girls in our area.'

With the money he earned, he had already married off two of his sisters. The third one's alliance was already fixed. Whenever the vehra folks sat down to draw up a list of sensible young men, Finnah's name would always figure at the top. He had shouldered the responsibility of his entire family. 'Whose son actually thinks like this these days?'

'Who thinks?' Melu's bapu repeated these words, as he entered his kothri. 'He addresses even a far-removed stranger in a respectful manner, and greets everyone with utter humility. Such sons are born only to the fortunate ones. They aren't born in every other family, after all.'

Talking to himself in this manner, when Melu's bapu went and sat down on the manji set out in the sun, he kept discussing Finnah with Dyalo for a very long time. Feeling embarrassed, Dyalo kept saying, 'hoon-hanh'. Every time he mentioned Finnah's name, scared of revealing her innermost thoughts, Dyalo would simply give her bapu a sidelong glance, in a bid to assess his response.

Almost a year before Finnah had joined the army, one day he and Dyalo had run into each other in Partapa's fields. Almost like a child, he had asked her, very spontaneously, 'Dyalo, you... you, too, join the army with me. No?' At the time, Dyalo was barely thirteen or fourteen years old, and Finnah was five or six years her senior. On hearing this crazy idea, Dyalo had laughed so much that she hadn't been able to stop for a long time. On seeing a dimple on Dyalo's right cheek, formed by her hysterical laughter, Finnah had smiled to himself.

'You're really the grandfather of all the crazy ones!' This is what Dyalo had said as soon as she had stopped laughing. 'Do girls ever join the army, you crazy fellow?'

But Finnah had, again, spoken with his characteristic naivety 'Why ever not? Girls drive motorcycles and cars these days. They pilot planes, too, and you say they can't join the army?'

Dyalo always found such talk on his part somewhat strange. He would always read out such stories from the newspapers and from books to the people living in the vehra. As he had studied up to class five, he was regarded as the most qualified young boy in the entire vehra. But when he discussed such things with Dyalo, she always thought he was being naive. That is why, thinking back to what he had said, she had kept smiling to herself, as she lay on her manji that night. And when she had met Finnah after many days, reminding him of his idea of joining the army, she had teased him no end. This had left him so deeply embarrassed that thereafter, he had not been able to face Dyalo for several days.

Today, when Finnah visited their house, Dyalo had suddenly been reminded of that incident. She had stuffed her chunni into her mouth and gagged her laughter somehow. Then she asked him, somewhat sheepishly, 'Bhai, do you live in Dilli, now?'

'It's quite far from Dilli, nearly eight hundred miles away. By train, it takes two days to get there. It's a very strange place. Men and women chew their words and speak.' Then, once again, he had started telling her the same kind of stories that he used to narrate to other people before joining the army.

Dyalo did like him a great deal. Now on hearing bapu praise him, she had temporarily forgotten how bharjai and her nephews had visited them like strangers and left, something that had rankled in her mind for a long time. While reflecting on her childhood memories, some of which were bound up with Finnah, she was suddenly reminded of Melu, who had become a stranger despite living under the same roof. For months on end, he would not visit them. Coming in late, he would merely spend the night and leave the next morning, in the pre-dawn hours, as if he didn't wish to come face to face with anyone. But each time Finnah came home, dumping his holdall and trunk at home, he would immediately set off to pay his respects to the elders in the community. Even today, though he had been home barely a couple of hours, he went to call on virtually everyone, made enquiries about Dharma, and then left for the town.

'There is no dearth of goodness in this world,' Melu's bapu continued to talk, as though to himself, 'Now, just see, he is no blood relation of theirs. Rather, Dharma's son had once picked a fight with his father. But he is such a good person that when he came home on leave, and learnt about it, he went straight to Dharma and said, "Now chacha, do tell bhai not to use such language in future. Why should he? Is my father not related to him? So, if he speaks ill of him, won't he feel embarrassed, too?" Just look at this, such satyugi people also exist in this kalyug.'

It was as if Melu's bapu had forgotten everything else, and all he could remember now was Finnah.

It was late afternoon. When Dyalo asked Melu's bapu if he wanted some rotis, he was still caught up in his thoughts and said, 'If there is any, then give it to me. You don't have to make it afresh now. I'm not hungry, really.'

Dyalo handed over a roti and a half that was leftover. Seeing two chunks of molasses on top, he first thought of asking her how much dough was left, but then the moment his eyes fell upon the firewood near the chulha and a few sticks of cotton plants lying in the courtyard, he asked, 'Putth, didn't your bebe get these dry sticks yesterday?'

'Yesterday, she was saying that Partapa hadn't started harvesting his cotton yet. She'll bring them today.'

'But how will we burn the wet ones she brings from Partapa? She is crazy. Why couldn't she get a bundle from someone else?'

'Tomorrow, I will go. I'll go and get the dry ones from someone. Two bundles will see us through for ten days or so.'

Again, Melu's bapu's face fell. When he used to work as a daily wager, they had never felt the dearth of dry firewood. Punnan, the mate who used to take care of the canal, was an old friend of his. Whenever he needed some firewood, his friend would fell a keekar and bail him out. Now in the winters, his body just didn't have enough strength to let him work; he barely managed to look after himself.

'All right then...you don't worry. If God permits, I'll go with you tomorrow.' It was as if he was trying to reassure Dyalo.

After eating his roti, he lay down on the manji once again. Carrying a chunni in her hand that she had begun embroidering the previous year, Dyalo came and sat next to him on a brick. Straightening her chunni out, she started looking at the small, floral design, embroidered in pale, yellow-coloured thread, in such a way as though she was reminding her bapu of her daaj. On seeing the chunni, Melu's bapu wanted to ask her something, but then he turned his face away from the sun. After a while, lying on the manji, his face covered with a khes, he had started taking long deep breaths, as though he was trying to push out something stuck inside his chest. His breathing was, in fact, becoming harder.

Lost in her own thoughts, Dyalo had started embroidering the incomplete floral design on the chunni. Each time she pulled the needle through her chunni, with an audible jarring sound, she felt as though her bapu's breathing was slowing down further. But Dyalo was not looking in his direction.

'Bapu.' After some time, she called out to him loudly, as if she was shouting for him somewhere out in the wilderness.

'Hanh!' Startled, Melu's bapu took the khes off his face, and asked, 'Putth, what is the matter?'

For a long time thereafter, Dyalo couldn't think of anything to say. Surprised, he had kept looking at Dyalo; but she was lost in her thoughts, again, as she went about moving the needle in and out of her chunni, somewhat mechanically.

'What is the matter, putth?' Melu's bapu asked in a somewhat impatient manner.

Still Dyalo didn't utter a single word. But after a while, feeling somewhat embarrassed, she said, 'I was…I was saying that, bhai, let all of us go to the town, now…'

She hadn't quite finished saying what she was, when Melu's bapu also fell silent in the same way in which she suddenly had, and started looking towards the sky. Dyalo also didn't speak a word more. It was as if their mutual silence was now fanning out like fog, enveloping them. So much so that they couldn't even see each other, very clearly. Then after a very long time, it was Dyalo who broke the silence.

'Now why are we all sitting here?' When she put this solemn question in a spontaneous manner, the way a wise person often does, Melu's bapu felt a lump rise in his throat. But Dyalo spoke again, 'If you were working as a siri for someone, it may have been an obstacle. But now that we live off our own resources, we'd be much better off there. Besides, the way bhabhi's brother was saying, our Melu bhai might have taken some big house on rent there. Now what is left for us here?'

He felt as though each word of Dyalo's was corroding his guts, like mercury. The fog before his eyes became denser and the sky appeared dark and inky.

That very moment, when some commotion was heard outside, Melu's bapu got up with a start, and said, 'What has happened now!'

Lurching forward, Dyalo saw a big crowd of people approaching their house from the direction of the dharamshala. Long before they reached Dyalo's house, many other women of the vehra had gathered around them. In the cacophony that followed, nothing was clear. Certainly, something was brewing. Gathering her chunni and putting it away on the wrong end of the manji, she said, 'I will go and find out.'

Rising from the manji in a hurry, Melu's bapu said, 'No, putth, you don't go, I will go.'

Dyalo found this kind of behaviour on the part of her bapu somewhat strange. She looked at his face and felt as though its glow had died in a minute. More than the commotion outside, it was the 'dhak-dhak' of her own heartbeat that Dyalo could hear very clearly now. Without even casting a glance towards her, bapu simply gathered his khes and set off towards the dharamshala.

As Dyalo peeped out of the door, she saw Bogha's mother beating her chest, wailing and screaming loudly. Then suddenly, she started running towards the village, spouting abuses at whoever came her way. By the time she had reached the village well, two women had caught hold of her. She kept beating her chest in the same violent manner, calling out the names of someone's sons and abusing them, shaking her head in a violent manner like a crazy woman, trying her best to wriggle out of the grasp of the two women and flee. Her chunni and one of her juttis lay a little short of the well, in the tracks left by a horse cart. Half of her scattered gray hair had fallen all over her face, on account of which she looked almost like a witch. After a while, when she saw two men leave the congregation and come towards them, she wriggled out of the grip of those two women and ran towards the village. As the women were still tugging at her kurta, it split up to her armpit, and hung loose. One of the men who had followed her grasped her firmly from behind, and both of them dragged her away to her house. Following close on their heels, the entire crowd also proceeded towards Bogha's house.

Dyalo could still hear the shouts and screams of Bogha's mother. 'Weh, may all your three sons die! May God make you lose everyone, so that not even a single person survives to light a deeva! You come to me, and I'd swallow you alive, weh, you demons of yore! I spit on you, you stubborn ones. I spit on you.'

It was a dreadful voice. Squirming inside, Dyalo plugged

her ears with her chunni. She couldn't stand by the door, any longer. Trembling in fear, she went and lay down on the manji. After some time, the commotion began to die down. She felt as though Bogha's mother's wailing had also subsided somewhat.

Then Dyalo heard the footfalls of her bapu, and instantly, she sat up on the manji. She could sense that bapu was out of breath. His eyes lowered, he came in and sat on the manji, and the moment he did so, an incessant bout of coughing began. Dyalo didn't ask him a thing. Simply getting up from there, she went and sat on the same brick again.

'What will become of this world?' slumping down on the manji, he asked as soon as he had caught his breath again.

'What's the matter, bapu?' Now Dyalo's voice sounded more composed.

'What do you think is the matter? These bloody rascals have come into some money, and now they go around preening.'

'Who are you talking of?'

'This, Taroo Singha, who else? In the morning, these people might have seen Bogha's footprints in their cotton fields. He was busy watering his fields when these buggers started dragging him into their trolley, saying, "Hanh, hanh, he is the one who stole our cotton at night". Bheeta has come from the fields, and he was saying, "All the three sons of Taroo kept hitting him in the trolley as they drove right up to the canal." Each time he abused, the elder one would jump at his throat, hit him hard in the ribs, and say, "Now tell us, at what rate did you sell the cotton?" Oh…oho! Have you ever heard of such brutality? Oye stupid fellows, even if that poor man has made a mistake, does it mean you should go to the extent of killing him? Compassion has completely dried up in human beings, but God watches everyone. At least you should fear Him, if nothing else. Oh…

oho…! What times have we fallen on? Waheguru, Waheguru! All right, Sacche Patshah, it's all up to you, now!' While talking in this manner, he was racked by such a paroxysm of coughing all of a sudden that he couldn't even breathe for some time. Dyalo felt as though the earth was revolving upside down. She felt as though her chunni lying towards the wrong end of the manji was also floating in the air.

Melu's bapu was now being racked persistently by bouts of coughing. It was as if his entire body was being winnowed. Still coughing badly, he was sitting up on the manji. It had made no difference to the intensity of his cough, though. Dyalo got up and went towards the chulha to light the fire—she knew very well that now her bapu wouldn't be able to pull himself off the manji unless a few drops of tea had seeped inside him.

As she was about to light the chulha, she was again reminded of the firewood. But seeing bapu's condition, she didn't have the heart to say anything to him. She took a dung-cake out of the many bebe had stored away. Breaking up the small, dry sticks of a bushy weed, she pushed them into the chulha. Then as she was breaking the dung-cake into smaller pieces to scatter them over the sticks, she discovered that the cake was damp at the core. The bushy weeds did catch fire, but the pieces of dung-cake remained unlit. Crushing them, as she thrust two more sticks into the chulha, the entire courtyard was flooded with smoke.

Melu's bapu's cough had become worse now. He would only get some relief if he was given a cup of hot tea, soon. Dyalo had put the water on to boil. After breaking the dry cotton twigs and bushy weeds and thrusting them all into the chulha, she was blowing over them, but the fire would smoulder for a while and then die down. With the clouds of smoke becoming denser, her eyes had begun to water. As she wiped her eyes repeatedly, they were now beginning to hurt her.

'You, bhai...' Melu's bapu wanted to say something, but his insistent cough would simply not let him speak a word. Oblivious to him, Dyalo was busy lighting the fire, but it simply wouldn't burn steadily. While rubbing her smoke-filled eyes, Dyalo, once again, heard the shouts and screams of Bogha's mother. Startled, she was up on her feet. On going to the rear side, next to the barbed wire, when she tried to gauge the situation, she found that along with her screams, the riotous commotion of the people was also rising. The voice of Paloo, the old man, could clearly be heard from a distance. Many other people were also shouting and screaming at the top of their voices.

'Bapu, it appears the people have returned from the town,' Dyalo said as soon as she came back.

But Melu's bapu was still racked by coughs. With his tear-filled flaming-red eyes popping out, he looked at her as though he hadn't really heard anything she said. Coughing yet again, he lay down on the manji.

On seeing bapu in such a state, Dyalo really felt helpless. Seated in front of the chulha, this time, when she put some pieces of bushy weeds and cotton twigs into it, and blew over them, they caught fire. When she went in to get some molasses and tea leaves, Bogha's mother's screams and the accompanying commotion had become even more feverish. This commotion continued, unabated, till the tea had started boiling. Slowly, the noise began to fade away.

After some time, when Dyalo was about to pour tea into a katora, her hands trembled, and as a result, much of it spilled on to the floor. Surprised, she looked at her trembling hands. She took the katora to bapu, and her hands were still trembling.

'Bapu...tea.' As she said this, she felt as though there was fear in her voice too.

Taking the khes off his face, Melu's bapu looked at her, momentarily, as though he was looking at some stranger, trying to figure out who it was. But the very next moment, he spoke to her in a voice dripping with emotion, 'Putth, who will look after you once your bapu is gone?'

And Dyalo found it extremely difficult to keep standing there next to bapu. Uncontrollably, her tears had now begun to roll down her face.

Melu's bapu had barely had a sip or two of tea when Melu's bebe came in, breathless, a bundle of dry cotton sticks on her head. Dumping the bundle in the rear portion of the courtyard, when she threw the sickle down, it hardly reached as far as the bricks near the manji. Without even covering her head, as she came and sat in front of Melu's bapu, she turned her head around, left and right, thumped both her knees, and then peering at him hard, she said, 'Waheguru!... Have some mercy on us!... Sacche Patshah! We should always fear your Design!... What was happening, yesterday...and today...'

But as she was out of breath, she couldn't complete what she wanted to convey. The pale dread on her face made her look somewhat older, even uglier, to him. He had rarely seen her so frightened and scared. Gathering Dyalo's chunni up, she was looking towards her in a somewhat curious manner, as though she couldn't muster enough courage to recognize either the daughter or the father.

'Melu's bapu, what will become of this world?' After heaving a deep sigh, she slapped her forehead, almost involuntarily.

For a while, she fell silent, and then started off as if she was now talking mainly to herself. 'You see for yourself, how many bundles of sarson there are? Throughout the day, I was struggling in the cotton fields, with dry cotton plants tearing my flesh, and this is about all I've been able to gather. They have left us nothing—simply taken it all away. While coming back, as I plucked four bundles of sarson for saag, and two bundles of sarson shoots for the cattle, he says, "Hanh, hanh! Who are you to touch this?" He came towards me, hollering. And then he started foaming at the mouth, saying, "You have ruined our sarson." I, too, got angry and said, "Weh, innocent one! I'm as old as your mother! Do you have any shame left in you? This is not the way to behave!" He says, "It's you who ruins our fields, and then you expect us to feel ashamed!" … Heh…heh…weh, the craziest of the crazy ones, what is there if I take two small bundles of sarson?... Tell me. You have no dearth of anything. You have three ploughshares to work with. These days, you go around driving that tractor, as big as a kotha. You bloody miser, what are you going to do with two bundles of sarson?... Oye, you ill-intentioned ones!'

After turning her face away, she slapped her forehead twice, heaved a deep sigh and then fell silent. As the storm raging inside her was pushing itself up against her throat, she started off again. 'We shouldn't even go towards the fields of these bloody fellows. For two–two months, they don't pay us for winnowing. When they do settle the account, they deduct half the money. It's always their legs that are on top of our heads, and yet they claim, "We are the ones who give you work!" Bhai, if you give us work, it's hardly a favour to us. Don't you do it for your own selfish reasons?... These damned ones must be having more than a cartload of sticks. They might just be lying there until harh-jeth and go to waste, but these people wouldn't let you use them. Everything they do is a big favour. He was only doing a favour, as big as a cart, when he said, "Chachi, you may take it today, but in future, don't expect such favours. We also have a shortage of firewood." Weh, chandriyo, this godforsaken firewood is the same that people used to give away freely. It'd not only help clean up the place, but also earn them the blessings of the poor and needy. Such misfortune! What is happening to people, nowadays? Even the worms don't do that.'

Thereafter, she was suddenly reminded of something else. Forgetting everything else, she looked towards Dyalo and said, 'O kurre, for the time being, do we have enough flour for meals?'

Dyalo made no reply. Rather than engage with Dyalo's unspoken words, she changed the subject and said, 'I only learnt about that incident when I reached the fields. Dharma's children have been hungry since dawn. They must be in bad shape. Hey Waheguru! Who will repay such sinners? Throughout their lives, all they did was flay the entire family. They got them to plant their orchards, weed wild field overgrowth, and now after selling off everything, God knows which palace they have gone off to. And here is this family, just rotting away. Oh God! Who has heard of such a thing, before?'

Despite everything, when Dyalo and Melu's bapu didn't utter a single word, Melu's bebe first pressed her knees to rise to her feet, and then went and sat next to the bundle of dry cotton sticks. Loosening the rope, and pulling out two bundles of green grams, she handed them over to Dyalo and said, 'Grind this with salt and red chillies. I'll go and give it to those poor children. They could have it with their roti. How can they eat roti without a vegetable?'

Placing the saag on the ledge next to the chulha, Dyalo

went straight in, without a word. Melu's bebe went ahead and sat on the same bricks. Then she smoothed out the crumpled layers of her darned salwar, and started dusting it off. On noticing three holes in it, she started fumbling over them as though she had only just spotted them. After wrapping herself into a warm shawl, she resumed talking in her usual manner.

The pitch of Bogha's mother's intermittent screams had again begun to soar. Her ears attuned to those sounds, Melu's bebe asked, 'O kurre, Santi's husband was not well. Could anything have happened to him?'

Melu's bapu maintained a studied silence and even Dyalo, after walking in, had busied herself with sowing or knitting to such an extent that there was no sign of her outside. The meaning of this mysterious silence on the part of both father and daughter had not dawned on her yet. Perhaps that's why she stepped out, saying, 'Let me go and find out what all this is about?'

Melu's bapu looked towards the door, but he didn't see Dyalo anywhere. On coming in, she had decided to lie down on a manji, which had a pile of clothes stacked on it. As she lay there, gazing fixedly at the roof, her thoughts began to get tangled up, like the tricoloured threads of her embroidery, used in the daaj that had been made for her wedding. Two chunnis, one phulkari, two shoulder bags with peacocks on them, two durries, four khes and two pieces of cloth her brother Melu had bought her for the suits. She wanted to open the old trunks and rummage through them, looking for all this, but she didn't have enough strength to rise to her feet. She felt as though all her energy had been drained out, leaving her body completely listless.

Then she remembered all those shops in town, which she

had seen once, stocked with a wide range of coloured threads and materials. Who knows where those shopkeepers managed to get such stocks from?

Outside, she thought she heard Finnah talking to her bapu. The moment she heard his voice, her heart began to beat much faster. Feeling a sudden burning sensation in her chest, she got up and came out. That is when she learnt that it wasn't Finnah, but Labhu, the 'lord of creation', who was sitting with her bapu. Wiping one of his big eyes with the corner of his turban, and shaking his head in the way in which a goat often does while munching something, he seemed to be busy discussing some very serious matter with him.

Dyalo couldn't think of anything to say. Settling down next to the chulha, she started grinding the saag of green grams. While grinding the saag, the moment her eyes fell upon half a cup of tea left in the bowl, she wondered why she hadn't offered it to bebe. The poor woman was really very exhausted. But it was now as cold as water. When would she heat it up and when would she drink it?

'O kurre, are you going strong, daughter?' Labhu suddenly looked at her and asked, wiping his sunken eye.

'Aho, tayya.'

Who knows whether or not Labhu had heard her response, but turning his attention from her, he had already started talking to her bapu in his characteristic soft, feminine voice. 'If you wish to send something to town, give it to me. I'll start for the town, early in the morning. Do you hear me?… Aho!'

Startled, Dyalo looked at him, and then pricked up her ears to overhear their conversation.

After mouthing off something in his characteristic, nonchalant manner, Labhu spoke in a rather conspiratorial tone, 'I'm thinking very seriously of going to the town now. What is left for us, here? One of my nephews lives there. He has kids, too. It'll keep me busy... Now...bhai...I can't get myself to work, anymore. You know, ever since he has given up liquor, he keeps pestering me. My nephew says, "Tayya, why do you suffer for nothing? Why don't you come and live with us, and eat what we eat. Bhai, you aren't going to make too many demands on us in any case. All you do is sit quietly in a corner, eat whatever little you need to, and keep chanting Ram's name." What say you, bhai? I somehow don't feel like going there. You are a wise man, and you know very well that even if he is simple and naive, once your son is married off, even his mother will not be able to put up with him...then how can I? Henh, tell me, am I not right, bhai? But when I take a long-term view of it, I feel, I can't manage on my own...so I may have to go, ultimately. And there is no escape from it. Who will take care of me here? After all, they have to look after me...regardless of whether they are good or not... Hundred or two hundred kilos of wood is all they would need for me. They'll have to carry my dead body, out of shame... Now, what say you, it's not the panchayat members who are going to carry me away, after all. Henh, bhai, am I saying the right thing or not?'

Wiping his dusty and dishevelled grey moustache with a corner of his turban, when Labhu broke into a toothless grin, his mouth looked somewhat like that of a lizard, gaping. Looking towards him, Dyalo couldn't help breaking into laughter. Doubling over, she said, 'Come on, tayya, what makes you think that here we don't have enough people to carry you off?'

That moment, Labhu became very serious. Breathing deeply, he said, 'Come on, putth, there is no such thing. I'm not a stranger to you. I was just repeating what my nephew says. Besides, putth, now I'm at the end of my life. I can't do a spot of work. Baccha, now I'll have to spend the rest of my life holding on to someone's knees, no? Am I not right, bhai?'

As Labhu didn't have any relatives living in the village, he would come to their house every third or fourth day, and unburden himself. The nephew in town, whom he often mentioned, was only distantly related to him, from the third or fourth generation of his grandfather's chacha or tayya.

Ever since Dyalo was a child, she had seen no change in Labhu whatsoever; the same frail body and a crooked turban with a long trail, khaddar kurta, and khaddar wrap-around, pulled tight over his calves. His juttis were always old and worn out, stitched at several places. It's not that he couldn't buy a new pair; but he had a knack of converting a brand new pair of juttis into an old one. Every two months or so, he would get his turban starched, a particular habit of his that had made him the constant butt of social ridicule.

'Did you say you were planning to leave late, this very night?' Melu's bapu asked him, reminding him of what he had suggested earlier.

'Hanh, I'll leave after I have had my roti, say, around ten or eleven.'

'Why, in such cold weather? Do you have to settle some account on priority?'

'No, it's something else.' Labhu spoke in a muffled voice, as if trying to keep a secret. While speaking, he ran the loose end of his turban over his eye.

'Why, what's the matter? Are you carrying someone's "opium"?'

Labhu looked first towards the left, then the right, and

finally edged closer to Melu's bapu. Peering into his eyes, he spoke in a low voice, 'Just load it in, this is what it is. You know that Sauna bania. I've to carry two of his sacks, one of cotton and the other, of grains... Who knows what all he may have stuffed inside? He says I must carry them at night.'

'But if it's something illegal and you get caught, you'll land in jail. He won't lose anything.'

'I'll name him straightaway. Why should I lie?'

'Do you have to marry off your sons that you're doing such things? Why can't you sit still and not do such things?'

The loose end of his turban still in his mouth, it looked as if Labhu was actually reflecting over the matter. After a while, he spoke in a low voice, 'You are right, in a way. But this is how I make a little extra money. It helps me earn a good living... You are wise yourself... I'm not in a position to load and offload things now. Some carry this sack in their trolleys, some on their horse carts, and the rest use camels for this purpose...what say you, bhai, what do we do, now? We are forced to lick the feet of the dead. You are wise. We, too, have to earn our keep, somehow. Bhai, so long as one is breathing, this body keeps demanding food. Henh, what do you say?'

Whenever Melu's bapu spoke in this manner, Labhu found it rather difficult not to react instantly. That was why, as he rose to his feet, he spoke mainly to mask his embarrassment, 'If you want to send something heavy, I'll come back, again, to find out. Let me first go and visit that seth for a while,' saying which he had barely gone up to the door, when he came back, as though he had remembered something very important. Moving closer to Melu's bapu, he spoke in a very secretive tone, 'You are a wise man. Don't broach it with anyone. You know, these days, people really ride a high horse. It's very difficult to say which way things might go. So one should be very careful.'

After Labhu had left, once again, a hushed silence fell upon the house. Melu's bapu covered his face with a khes. Dyalo, who had been busy chopping saag, now sat with her head resting upon her knees, lost in her thoughts. (Perhaps, she was thinking of Finnah once again.) On seeing the dust kicked up by the feet of people returning from the fields, and hearing the commotion the children made, when she raised her head to look towards the well, she saw that the sunlight was falling short of the upper terraces of the houses. The thought of cooking roti uppermost in her mind, she walked into the kitchen, with hurried steps. But on seeing the gunny sack, she stopped in her tracks. It was empty. She came back out as quickly as she had walked in.

'Bapu,' she called out in a rather weak voice, 'Should I go get flour from the shop?'

'Henh?' Startled, her bapu first took the khes off his face, and then spoke, looking towards her, 'Flour?'

Standing silently, Dyalo was waiting for his answer, but he kept staring at the sky with vacant eyes, as if he couldn't really think of anything to say. After a while, she silently walked in, and started rummaging through the containers for the last few grains. There was a small quantity of wheat in one container, and about two sers of maize in the other. The other containers were empty. But she couldn't have taken the wheat or maize out of the containers without her bebe's permission, and gone to the shop to have it ground. Who knew which mounds her bebe was busy climbing now! She hadn't returned yet. This thought had barely crossed her mind when bebe came charging in, blabbering.

'Melu's bapu, have you heard this?' She was nearly breathless as she came closer, widening her eyes, 'I was surprised when I heard this—they say Taroo's sons have dragged Bogha to the police station.' Without waiting for a response from Melu's bapu, she kept talking agitatedly, repeating everything that Melu's bapu had already heard about Bogha. She elaborated on how this news had left Bogha's mother completely distraught. Suddenly, in the middle of it all, she thought of Dharma's children and that moment, looking towards Dyalo, who was standing in the doorway, her face half-covered with her chunni, she said, 'O kurre, I told you that there is enough flour. So you quickly roll out two rotis for me. You're standing as if it's someone else's house.'

'What do I cook with? My head?' On hearing Dyalo speak in this irritated, almost exasperated manner, all the signs of agitation suddenly vanished from her bebe's face. Her demeanour changed and deep furrows appeared on her forehead. But she spoke in a somewhat restrained manner, saying, 'O kurre, why are you sounding so exasperated? You take the maize that is lying in the container and get it ground in Nandu's machine. Who else can I ask for help now? Go my dear daughter, be wise and attend to it.'

Dyalo went back in, as exasperated as before. Her mother started off on the same story. But the moment she heard Shinda's wailing from outside, she threw an embroidered shawl over her shoulders and coming out, hollered, 'Now what's happened to you?'

But the moment Shinda set his eyes upon her, he started wailing all the more loudly. Edging away from her but looking at his bebe with fearful eyes, Shinda was signalling towards the she-calf and trying hard to convey something, but his long bout of crying had parched his throat so much that the words were stuck there. His eyes were streaming, and as he lifted his kurta to wipe them, they appeared swollen.

Seeing Shinda's condition, Melu's bebe became worried. As she came closer and looked at the she-calf, she nearly screamed, 'Oye, weh! You be damned. Look at the havoc these enemies of ours have inflicted on this poor creature.'

Both the hind legs of the calf were soaked in blood. On the right leg, a little below the knee, towards the inner side, almost four inches of skin had been flayed off, as though someone had sliced it off with a sickle. As she was trying to gauge the extent of the injury, Shinda howled even harder. Shaking her head in a wild rage, she turned back and rushing towards Shinda, standing in a corner, she kicked him in the shins, and screamed, 'Hai weh, may you be ruined, you enemy of mine! Why did you have to show such bitterness towards this poor calf?'

On being kicked, Shinda went running towards the house, howling with all his strength. Standing next to the chulha, Dyalo instantly threw her shawl around him, enveloping him. While Melu's bebe was busy abusing the calf, trying to push him home, Chanda, the lame one, who was herding his goats home, stopped to speak to her in a composed manner, saying, 'Why are you getting angry with your son? First find out what happened. Why are you making his life miserable? As it is, this poor fellow has been beaten up so severely. And here you go charging at him, again.'

When Melu's bebe twisted around to look at Chanda, she started staring at his dust-laden face, his bushy beard and his half-leg as though she had, in her nervous agitation, committed some serious error of judgement.

'Bacchittar's son attacked its legs with a spade. And tell me, how is this little one responsible for it?' Chanda spoke, looking towards the calf's injured leg. 'He was going to hit the hooves, but it's the ankle that took the brunt.'

'Why the hell did my father's brother-in-law hit this one with a spade?' said Melu's bebe, trembling with rage, as she desperately tried to hold on to her embroidered shawl, which was slipping off, while pushing the calf ahead. 'Did she graze on his grape climbers?'

'It has nothing to do with grazing.' Using a stick to guide one of his goats that had wandered off towards the well, Chanda spoke in his usual composed manner, 'He was grazing the calf when, by mistake, it sauntered into their wheat fields. He was trying to bring it back, when that fellow hit him in the shins with a stick, and hit the calf's ankles with a spade, no less than three or four times.'

The moment Melu's bebe heard this, it was as though all her clothes had been set on fire. Without thinking of the consequences, she began to hurl abuses at Bacchittar's entire family. Bacchittar's house was only three houses away, a little ahead of the well. Her screams could be heard clearly in their house. But it seemed as if, at that moment, she couldn't care less about any damned fool. While chivvying the calf home, she kept rambling on, saying whatever came to her mind.

After seating Shinda next to the chulha, when Dyalo looked towards the calf stumbling in, with its head down, she was almost thrown off-balance. 'Hai nee, bebe, half of its leg is sliced off.'

'May his elders and his children also die! May death devour all his unborn ones, too!' Seething and simmering, when Melu's bebe walked the calf to the trough, Melu's bapu also got up from his manji and looked at the calf's legs, nervousness showing in his eyes.

But much before he could say something, a paroxysm of coughing racked his body.

Both Melu's bebe and Dyalo immediately got down to dressing the wound on the calf's leg. Pulling his kurta down to his knees, and wiping his eyes again and again, Shinda sobbed for a long time, intermittently stealing nervous glances at his bebe. One moment, he would look at his agitated bebe, and the very next, his eyes would go darting in the direction of his bapu, who was still racked by a coughing bout. Then as he pressed that part of his calf muscles, where he had been hit repeatedly by the stick, he felt as though the pain was slowly getting worse. After cleaning up the wound on the calf's leg, when Melu's bebe inspected it carefully, once again, the sight sent a shudder down her spine. It appeared as though his bone, too, had been cut a little. Her low, moaning voice became high-pitched, once again. While dressing the wound, she kept blabbering in her characteristic manner.

The light had retreated from the terraces of the houses and the glow of the setting sun was slowly dissolving into a haze of darkness. Melu's bebe was thinking of the many things that she still had to do. She had to go to Kirpal's house and get a kilo or two of wheat chaff for the calf and the heifer. She now had to go to the machine herself to get the grains ground. As the machine was on the outskirts of the village, she couldn't possibly have sent Dyalo at such an odd hour. She was to carry roti for Dharma's children. That's why, as soon as she had finished dressing the calf's wound, she walked in, still muttering under her breath. Tying a handful of maize into a corner of her shawl, and picking up a torn khes for the wheat chaff, as she was about to leave, she ordered Dyalo, 'If there is some molasses left, give it to the calf.' She knew perfectly well that, forget about leaving something for their heifer, there wasn't enough molasses in the house to even sweeten their morning tea.

The moment her mother stepped out, Dyalo came back to Shinda, who was staring at her with tear-stained eyes. She wiped his eyes clean with a corner of her chunni, and said, 'No, no, don't cry, my little brother! Did you also get hurt somewhere?'

'He hit me here with a spade, twice.' Lifting the kurta off his wound, he touched his calf muscles, and then pointing to his back, he spoke in a tremulous voice, 'He hit me here, as well.'

Dyalo saw that his calf muscle was marked by a weal. His legs and feet had been bruised badly, pricked by all kinds of thorns and twigs. Fighting her emotions, she spoke in a heavy voice, 'Don't worry. Those chandriyas will die of worms. Come, I'll take you inside. Lie down, with a khes over your head, while I make tea for you... All right?'

Gently holding his arm, she led him inside, made him lie down on a manji and covered him with a khes. By the time she had returned to the door, she suddenly thought of her bapu. He was still coughing harshly. Dyalo felt as though something was boiling inside her, and in spite of herself, she broke down. Stuffing a corner of her chunni in her mouth, she tried to force her tears from spilling over, and on the pretext of collecting the saag she had already cut, she started fumbling around on the floor. She couldn't gather the courage to look at her bapu. Slowly, while stoking the ashes in the chulha, as she started thrusting small pieces of dung-cake into it, with the idea of making tea for Shinda, her eyes brimmed over, and she broke down all over again. Then turning her face towards the wall, she wiped her tears. But her throat had turned so bitter as though she had chewed an acacia shoot.

When Melu's bapu got some respite from his coughing, he lay down again. But that very moment, he heard a commotion filtering in from the dharamshala, almost as if the panchayat had returned from the town. He made a bid to get up, but fell back as though the cough had sapped all his energy. He simply could not get up, but as the commotion increased by the minute, his anxiety, too, mounted. Suddenly, he felt as though some people had started squabbling. That is when he pushed himself up on his elbows and rose to his feet.

'Dyalo, bhai, go and see, what's the matter?' he spoke, a picture of anxiety.

But Dyalo just went across to the window, looked towards the dharamshala, and as she turned away, all she said was, 'I don't know, bapu.'

On hearing her detached voice, when Melu's bapu looked at her somewhat surprised. She was, at that time, looking for a stout piece of wood, rummaging through the bundle her mother had brought in. With the support of the long, wooden arm of the manji, he got up, took a few deep breaths and then slowly started walking towards the door. When he came out and looked towards the dharamshala, peering into the glare of artificial lights, it seemed to him that a large crowd had assembled outside. He recognized the voices of the panch and Pala, too. That very moment, he ran into Finnah.

'So bhai, what happened, then?' Melu's bapu asked in an excited, though breathless, voice.

'Nothing really! What did you expect, henh?' Finnah was speaking in an unusually hurried tone. 'Neither the sarpanch nor any other responsible person from the village was there. We wore ourselves out unnecessarily, and came back, frustrated.

DC sahab says, "I have no time for you." When we met the SDM, he just turned up his nose and said, "Today, rickshaw wallahs are taking out a procession, so I'm on duty there." We never saw the police officer. There was another officer, with a bushy beard like a wire mesh. He was the only one who heard us out, but said, "I'll make sure that DC sahab gets to see your petition. Whatever is his hukam, I'll convey it to you. I can do nothing more than that." We kept sitting there until the evening, and then, we neither saw him nor any other officer. Finally, we came back, exasperated.'

'Did you secure Dharma's release or not?' Melu's bapu asked Finnah with genuine concern, ignoring the other details.

'How could we secure his release?' Finnah responded, his anger turning into anguish, 'We met the thanedaar, who said, "Bhai, I arrested them under Section 751. Ask some responsible villagers to stand surety for them, and then take them away. On your request all I can do is to file the challan today itself. Nothing beyond that." If the people of the village go, and some officer agrees to meet them, then things could be worked out, not otherwise. No? Now, where else could we look for help? The officer who grants the bail is busy with the rickshaw wallahs' strike.'

'Was there no other way of resolving this?'

'They say, you sink only if you are unable to breathe, no?' Finnah spoke somewhat testily, 'When our own people didn't set out from the village, who would have bothered about us, there? Chacha, what do I tell you? This matter is now a bad tangle. Anyway, I'll go early tomorrow morning and meet the DC. They have strict instructions to listen to the complaints of army personnel,' he said and went home.

For a while, Melu's bapu remained in a dilemma, and then

he too simply returned home, lacking the courage to press the matter any further.

After putting the tea to boil on the chulha, Dyalo walked indoors. That very moment, a sudden flame leapt out, as a dry piece of wood had caught fire. Melu's bapu first looked at the rising flame and then as he was sitting down on the manji, his attention was claimed by the calf's wounded leg. The calf stood, eyes closed, dispirited and exhausted. It was constantly shaking its wounded leg to ease the pain. For a while, he felt very strongly about the calf's pain, almost as if it was his own. But after some time, it was as though his feelings had suddenly died. Though the calf was still in front of him, now looking at its swollen leg and open wound, he couldn't empathize at all, or feel his heart stir.

Just then, an unexpected sound—a shot fired from a double-barrelled rifle—startled Melu's bapu out of his stupor. At the same time, he heard someone yelling threats, from the direction of the hills, close to the kassi. And then a sudden hush descended upon the other side of the dharamshala. That very moment, Finnah came out of his house, and looking towards the hills, said, 'Chacha, it looks as though some trouble is brewing, where Wadhawa Singh's fields are.'

'It looks as though Dharma's sons are protesting,' Melu's bapu nodded in agreement.

'Dharma's sons?' Finnah looked at him in utter disbelief, 'Are you in your senses, chacha? They have been in jail for so many days now. Throughout the day, we were knocking around, trying to secure their release. How could they have arrived so soon? They couldn't have dropped from the sky.'

Melu's bapu found it strange that the thought of Dharma's sons should hit him all of a sudden. Near the dharamshala, complete silence prevailed.

'Oye! Which "brother-in-law" of mine dares to do this? If you want to live, then come out into the open... Oye!' When Melu's bapu heard this war cry, coming from the direction of the hills, he felt as though Modhu's neem tree had begun to shed leaves.

Finnah, too, heard the same shout, but he merely said, 'Now, who is this one?' and the next moment, he went bounding towards the wilderness.

That very moment, Finnah's mother came out muttering, and stood where he had stood. It was as if she was trying to say something for the benefit of Melu's bapu, 'Look at him. He is such a fool. Ever since he arrived, he hasn't even had a cup of tea at home. Now again he's gone off. Someone should ask him, bhai, what will you get by singeing your hands? Who knows who's there? Look at the way he is going around, feeling important... These days, you can't really trust anyone. People get worked up over nothing. Look at the way they've treated Dharam Singh. Until the evening, the children were howling. Only a while ago, I went and gave them some roti-tuk. We still have to go and fetch our utensils. It's already dark. How can one be everywhere?'

Melu's bapu found her voice rather strange. Otherwise too, he felt as though he couldn't understand a thing she was talking about. And speaking in this manner, she went back towards her house. After bolting the door from the outside, she, too, went off in the same direction in which Finnah had gone. Melu's bapu felt as though she had simply taken a round of their house and had now come in through the back door. When he turned back, he saw Melu's bebe walk in, with flour wrapped in her shawl, and a small bundle of knick-knacks balanced on her head.

'O kurre, what is happening around us? What bad times have we fallen on? These damned ones are out to do their worst… Did you ever hear of such a thing? He tells me, "Take it if you want to, or else go elsewhere." You son-beater, at least give me as much as I'm offering you; maize sells for a better price than wheat. May God bless us! He goes around with his tail between his legs. That bania is really the limit…he says, "Molasses will cost you one rupee and seventy five paisa a kilo. You buy if you want to buy, or else you go your way." Then he tells me that he'll accept only cash, and enter into no credit. Damned be his soul, where do they charge this rate? These people have no shame left in them. Henh! They are hell bent on overcharging you. They just want to skin you alive.'

Grumbling, she walked into the kothri. For some time, she kept hurling all kinds of accusations at Dyalo, as though preparing sweet tea had depleted their stock of firewood, tea leaves and molasses, completely. When Dyalo, too, responded in an equally terse and acerbic manner, she felt annoyed and came out of the kothri. The moment she stepped into the courtyard, she heard the war cries, again, followed by the screams of a woman and a gunshot in the distance. A sudden dread enveloped her, choking her.

'Waheguru, what has happened now, O, daughter of mine!' Though in her initial spurt of nervous agitation, she had walked up to the door, she retreated the moment she saw two young boys, armed with gandasas, coming from the direction of the dharamshala and running towards the wilderness, across the hills. And the pandemonium created by the people assembled inside the dharamshala was as if dacoits had already raided the village. When she saw three–four people walking quickly, trailing the young men with gandasas, she lurched forward to ask them, but before she could do so, they had moved on towards the wilderness. They, too, were carrying lathis and gandasas, and it appeared as though a fight had already broken out between the two warring factions.

Then suddenly Finnah's mother's howls and screams from the fields close by reached them. With the idea of asking Melu's bapu to protect himself from the cold outside, Melu's bebe admonished him gently, and then, throwing her shawl over her shoulders, as she stepped out of the door, saw Finnah's mother, shrouded in darkness, coming from the opposite side, beating her chest with both her hands. The moment she saw her in this condition, she felt she had lost her balance. Three or four women came out of Finnah's house, running, and encircled his mother instantly. Despite their repeated solicitations, Finnah's mother couldn't get herself to utter even a single word. Shouting, screaming, wailing and utterly disconsolate, she turned back, again and again, to look towards the wilderness as though her house, her family and all her possessions had been washed away by a flash flood. None could understand what could have transpired in such a short span of time. Seeing her in this condition, an unknown dread filled all the women. All she could say was, 'I have been robbed, O, my villagers! I've lost everything, O, the people of my village!'

While they continued to stand so, a man came rushing in from the wilderness, his feet pounding rather hard. His face and head were covered with a scarf, and he held a gandasa over his shoulder, firmly with both hands. Frightened by this sight, all the women retreated, slinking away towards the wall of Melu's house.

'Go, go. Rush back to your houses, now. No one should

stand here. Chachi, you too sit at home, and take it easy. Finnah bhaiji is all right. Don't make so much unnecessary noise,' said the man and rushed towards the dharamshala. As his face was covered, and his voice unfamiliar, no one recognized him.

But the moment she heard his words, they calmed Finnah's mother. Without a word, she simply sat on the ground. Then looking strangely at all those present, she asked, 'Who was that boy?'

'I think, he was Dheeru's younger one!' Melu's bebe suggested.

'You never know, he may have just said that to reassure me.'

'Don't worry, you'd better be strong. Go home now. Let the men find out everything on their own,' Chinni reassured her; and then all of them supported her and helped her walk across to Melu's house.

By this time, all the people who had assembled at the dharamshala had begun to disperse. They saw two of them go towards the sarpanch's house, and three–four of them, accompanied by that young man, proceed to the wilderness. And the rest simply went off towards the pond.

After reassuring Finnah's mother, the women saw her to her house. But seeing their mother's condition, Finnah's younger sister and two of his younger brothers suddenly burst into tears. It took Melu's bebe some effort to quieten them. Once all of them had settled down, they asked Finnah's mother to narrate what had happened. With half her attention still on the wilderness, from where the fading sounds of commotion were filtering in, she said, 'When I was following him, somewhere close to Kunda's fields, I felt as though someone…someone fired at him. Then I heard Finnah's yells. That moment, I thought he had fallen with a thud. Then I felt as if he was saying, 'Oye, you bastard, you've killed me.' Hai, hai, and then it was as though I had lost all my senses. I collapsed on the spot, right there.'

She had barely completed her story when they all heard shouts again. 'You run where you can now. I'll tell you...you bloody, son of a ...'

Again, they all shook with fear. Finnah's mother cried out, once, 'Hai, I'm dead, now...' and suddenly collapsed. She became hysterical. That very moment, her eyes rolled back and her limbs turned blue. Chinni went running across to the chulha, grabbed the tongs, and they had to struggle to break her spasms. She took a long time to open her eyes.

Suddenly, Melu's bebe broke into a heavy sweat and felt so uneasy that she could no longer stand. Without a word, she simply returned to her house. The moment she entered, she fell on the same manji that Melu's bapu had vacated. Though his cough had worsened, and the rasping of his breathing was audible, she couldn't get herself to go and check on him.

When Dyalo came by to pick out a few pieces of firewood from the bundle that was lying next to her manji, she, too, asked in a somewhat impersonal tone, 'Bebe, what is the matter?'

Rather than respond to her, all she said was, 'Henh, what did you say?' and then fell silent. Dyalo found her voice rather strange. She wasn't feeling too well herself, so she decided not to ask her, a second time, and carried the firewood to the chulha, by which she seated herself.

That moment, Melu's bebe felt as though thick, dark clouds of dust were gathering all around. First, she heard the sound of the wind screeching through the trees, and then that of the branches, breaking, collapsing and crashing...and also the thumping of the utensils, baskets, and other odds and ends toppling over the ledges; sounds that resounded in several courtyards. Nervous, she looked up at the dust-laden sky, and then covered her eyes with her shawl as if thick grains of sand had already clouded them.

After some time, Dyalo felt as though her mother was muttering something in her sleep. When she got up and went towards the manji, she heard her bebe, who had a shawl covering her face, mumbling something, none of which made any sense to her. She barely heard three or four sentences, 'Who knows, thirteenth day of his mourning may already be over.' 'Who bothers?' 'Man is not even worth what a cat or a dog is!'

'Nee, bebe, what's the matter?' Dyalo nervously shook her bebe by the shoulder.

Dyalo couldn't think of what to say next. Gripping her arm, and making her sit up, Dyalo said, 'Why don't you lie down inside.'

'Why, what is my problem, here?' Adjusting her chunni, bebe said, 'Is the storm still raging or has it blown over? Have you ever seen a dust storm in winter?'

'You'd better stand on your feet.' In a bid to suppress the emotional storm welling up inside her, it was as if Dyalo had mildly admonished her bebe, obliging her to stand up.

As she was supporting her and helping her move inside, Dyalo felt as though her bebe was trembling like a victim of Parkinson's. As she went in, she kept mumbling incoherently, only some of which made sense to Dyalo.

While she was helping her bebe lie down on the manji, Melu's bapu asked, 'What's the matter?'

'Nothing, what could be the matter? I was lying down outside, and she tells me, go and lie down inside. Now tell me, what's the big fuss about?'

Melu's bapu spoke somewhat tersely, 'What else? You mean

she should have strung up a swing for you there itself?'

With her head bowed, Melu's bebe came out, quietly. It was as though she was only waiting to be admonished by him. Pulling her quilt over her head, she lay down and pretended she had been asleep for hours.

After a while, when Melu's bapu asked, 'Oh! You had gone there? What was the matter? Did you find out something?' she made no effort to respond to him, at all.

Then he also fell silent. His breathing had grown difficult, again, perhaps, by yet another bout of coughing.

As Dyalo came in carrying the roti basket, she saw that the lantern, now down to its last reserves, was making a 'bhak-bhak' sound. After a while, a flame came leaping out of it, before dying away completely. Suddenly it was pitch dark and for a while at least, nothing was visible at all. It slipped her mind as to where the lantern was hanging. Putting the basket down, she edged closer to the wall in a bid to fumble across and locate it. And the moment she did so, her nostrils were instantly assailed by a strong stench of kerosene oil.

When all her efforts to light the lantern had failed, she came back. Shinda had got up and was seated ramrod straight on the manji. His face was still suffused with the pallor of an unknown fear. Staring at Dyalo, who was then trying to hang the lantern on a peg, he felt as though she was a ghost of some kind.

'Nee, bhaine, have you made some roti?' Though he had finally gathered the courage to ask her this, his eyes were focusing at the soot-laden chimney of the lantern.

'Hanh, I'll give it to you right away.'

Lantern in hand, as Dyalo retreated, her foot hit the basket, and the flour container toppled over.

'What happened?' startled out of his wits, her father asked. 'Nothing bapu.'

But her bapu's breathing had become all the more laboured.

She picked up the basket and put it on the ledge for utensils. She located the jar of the wild caper pickles and, sitting on the edge, started serving rotis.

Then suddenly it occurred to her that she had neither ground the green gram saag her mother had brought in, nor had she cooked the daal. Possibly, there was no daal. She couldn't have served wild caper pickle pieces, dripping with oil, to her bapu. The moment this thought hit her, she became all the more depressed.

'Bapu, you won't mind eating your roti with molasses?' she asked, diffidently.

Melu's bapu first coughed and then thought that even a little silence on his part could prove uncomfortable for Dyalo. He spoke somewhat reassuringly, 'Don't worry, putth. I'll have it dry, without anything. Just sprinkle a bit of salt on it. That might help my cough, too.'

Dyalo had no energy left in her to speak. When she was about to hand over two rotis to him, with two pieces of molasses from what her bebe had brought in, he asked, 'Have you given it to your bebe?'

'She is sleeping.'

Without a word more, Melu's bapu simply let her leave the rotis on his palm.

Dyalo handed two rotis to Shinda, with slices of wild caper pickle on top. When she saw that he, too, was looking for molasses, she explained to him through sign language that he could take it later. For some time, he just sat there, sulking, holding the rotis, but the moment Dyalo turned her back, he tore off chunks and began to eat.

Dyalo came back and sat down next to the container. Twice, she twisted around to look at her bebe, but didn't utter a single word. Bapu also didn't feel like pushing her again into waking her bebe, and giving her some roti. And Dyalo felt as if her tongue had stuck to her palate. Either because of this eerie silence or some other inexplicable reason, she felt sudden pangs, as though a centipede was rolling around inside her, scratching her innards with its prickly legs. The strange manner in which both bapu and Shinda were smacking their lips while eating made these pangs much worse. She felt suffocated, as though she had eaten thorny bers. Without asking them if they would like to have some more roti, she stepped out of the house.

The night was still young. Holding on to the pillar, next to the pond, she stood facing Finnah's house as though she were waiting for someone. For a while, she just stood there, staring into the void. The moment she heard sudden shouts from the wilderness, she started trembling. When she turned to look, Labhu was walking in with his camel, holding its nose string. For a moment, she continued to stare into the void, and then felt as though a swarm of locusts was emerging from the sky. The very next moment, she saw the same dark, intimidating shapes, closer. And then producing strange sounds of 'mansoo-mansoo', these shapes suddenly grew monstrously large and loomed overhead, the way monsoon clouds often dissolve and reassemble into all kinds of white and grey shapes. Dyalo could barely restrain herself from screaming, and felt the life ebbing out of her. Wrapping her chunni tightly over her head, she hurried back home.

Having had two rotis without the molasses, Shinda now lay on the manji, his head and face totally covered. Lying face up, bapu, too, was staring vacantly at the roof. The strange, eerie silence began to suffocate Dyalo, again. So much so, she couldn't bring herself to ask her bapu if he needed another roti. Picking up the basket, she put it on the ledge. That very moment, when a sudden knock sounded on the door, her bapu said, 'Putth, go and see, who it is.'

But before Dyalo could find out, he heard the strange 'khrap-kharp' of Labhu's juttis, and he simply lay there, waiting for him.

'So bhai, what have you decided?' The moment Labhu walked in, he wiped his eye with a corner of his turban; seeing the entire family lying so listlessly, and looking around, he approached the manji on which Melu's bapu lay.

'What happened? You're lying down?' he asked, in a bid to change the tenor of the conversation.

'Just like that…' While rising from the manji, Melu's bapu said, 'Are you leaving right away?'

'Hanh, I just have to load Lala's gunny sacks. The camel is waiting outside. So what have you decided?' Sitting at the foot of his manji, and casting a glance at Melu's bebe, who was lying listlessly, Labhu said, 'I was saying, bhai, why don't you come with me? We'll stay there, tomorrow. And if the boys are too busy, we'll come back in the evening. Who can stop us from coming back? Isn't it right, bhai? Henh? What's your name…?'

Melu's bapu had started coughing, all over again. Labhu waited, but got no answer. Seeing Melu's bebe lying, face and head completely covered, Labhu became somewhat suspicious, but he couldn't bring himself to ask if she was feeling well.

'Do you want tea or…?' Suddenly, Melu's bapu tossed a question at Labhu.

'Tea? Why, it will only delay us further. I was saying, why

don't we start now? Why wait?'

'No. It's nothing much. It's still quite cold. Besides, the night is still ahead of us. The distance is hardly twenty miles or so. It is not going to take us more than half an hour. Dyalo putth, why don't you boil some tea?'

The moment she heard her bapu's instructions, Dyalo set about preparing tea, though because she was still feeling restless, what she really wanted to do was to simply sit in a corner, all by herself.

Standing outside the door and masticating audibly, Labhu's she-camel appeared somewhat grotesque. Inside, Labhu had started spinning his never-ending stories. Despite the fact that Melu's bapu was nodding at what was being narrated, he was least interested in any of it. Immersed in his own thoughts, he was wandering in an entirely different world. He felt as though he had been stretched on a rack. He felt as if his legs were cracking like a branch of kareer. Stung by a sudden fear, he rose to his feet.

'What's the matter?' asked Labhu, disrupting his chain of thought.

'Nothing much! I'll be with you, soon.' Then after wrapping the khes around him, Melu's bapu let himself out the door.

'Tea is ready, bapu,' Dyalo said, noticing him as he stepped out.

Stepping closer to Dyalo, Melu's bapu asked her softly, 'So, then, do I go along with Labhu?'

It was as though Dyalo hadn't understood a word of what he said. Looking towards her bapu, she kept sitting there, her eyes wide in surprise. In the dim light of the chulha, her face seemed to have become almost unrecognizable.

'Henh, putth! What's your advice?' bapu asked, once again,

'Today, I have company, but you never know about tomorrow. There is no certainty. Henh?'

While she was pouring tea into the glasses, she felt as if she had lost her speech, once again, and her breathing, too, rasped.

'So, what do you suggest, putth?'

'You decide bapu. It's your wish.' With this, Dyalo felt a sudden lump in her throat.

'What is there to think about? If Melu suggests it, we'll all go and live with him there. Or else, I'll return with Labhu by tomorrow evening because what will I have to do there?'

Again, Dyalo couldn't think of anything to say, and after saying, 'All right', she fell silent. Melu's bapu also kept quiet for some time. Then he cleared his throat so as to ease his breathing, and said, 'If you say "No", I won't go.'

'Why not bapu? You go.' It was almost as if these words had escaped Dyalo, involuntarily.

But that very moment, bapu writhed as another coughing fit began. Holding his head, he sat, coughing his lungs out. Once he had recovered a bit, Dyalo handed him a glass of tea. On hearing him coughing persistently, Labhu also came out. Seated next to the chulha, and stoking the fire with a small piece of firewood, he said, 'So, you have consulted beebo? Bhai, to tell you honestly, now there is no reason for us to live in the village. I have decided that if the boys refuse to help, then we'll do manual labour and earn our money. Our limbs and eyes are still intact… Oye, simple one, there is hardly anyone left in the villages now. Every goon or lecherous man is masquerading as the Chaudhary. Am I not saying the right thing? Henh? Now what's left for us, here? Henh, bhai?'

Dyalo simply handed him a glass of tea and walked back in, without a word. She didn't want to nod assent to any of his suggestions. Slurping his tea, Labhu kept talking, but Melu's bapu didn't feel like responding to him.

As they rose to their feet, preparing to leave, Melu's bapu called out to Dyalo. When she came out, he asked her, once again, his voice dropping to an inaudible whisper, 'Putth, should I go along, then?'

'Hanh bapu, you go ahead.' This time round, Dyalo's voice was firm. She retreated inside and then handing him another khes, she said, 'Bapu, it's really very cold. You take this also.'

'It's hardly that cold today, bhai beebo.' Labhu was the one to butt in, 'I'm carrying an extra one with me. I'll give it to your bapu, if he needs it. Moreover, we'll be home in another two hours. Once you are home, it's no trouble, then. Henh?'

Without paying much attention to him, Melu's bapu wrapped the khes around himself tightly, and started walking. Then he returned from the middle of the courtyard. Dyalo was still standing next to the chulha. Edging closer to her, he spoke in a conspiratorial tone, 'Putth, don't tell your bebe about it. If she asks, tell her that the panchayat had asked for a meeting, and I've gone there. All right?'

Dyalo simply nodded her assent. That very moment, stuffing the corner of her chunni into her mouth, she started raising the wick of the sarson-oil lamp, resting in the alcove above the ledge; but as the oil was drying up fast, the lamp made odd 'chirrah-chirrah' sounds, and then the flame leapt up, unexpectedly, just once, before flickering weakly. Standing stock still, she kept staring at the flickering lamp. It was as if she lacked the courage to look in the direction in which her bapu had left.

Then suddenly, the light in the lamp faded away, as if someone had snuffed it out. In the dense, deepening darkness, when she looked around, her chunni stuffed into her mouth, she could see no one. On walking across to the door, when she peered towards the dharamshala, seeing a terrifying shape that resembled the grotesque shadow of Labhu's camel, she felt a sudden shudder deep inside. Watching her bapu hunched over and walking behind the camel, her heart began to pound. Her tears began to flow and her limbs grew numb. She lacked the energy to even stand there.

On negotiating the corner next to the dharamshala, once Labhu's camel had heaved out of sight, wiping her eyes with her chunni, Dyalo looked in that direction once again. Her bapu had stopped, and was now turning around to look back over his shoulder. Then, he too disappeared. Now, despite the light twinkling in one corner of the dharamshala, everything seemed to have dissolved into a blur of darkness, just the way it was for the one-eyed Giddhu. Her hands fumbling across the wall, she walked in stealthily, and sat down next to the chulha. Then covering her face and head with her chunni, she dropped her head between her knees. The sound of her wailing was now beyond her control.

Coming up to her, almost tiptoeing like a cat, and seeing her sitting in this state, bebe tapped her forehead sharply, saying, 'O kurre, the eternal mourner, what has stung you that you are crying your heart out in the middle of the night?'

Dyalo tried to calm herself, but failed. She broke into fresh wails. This annoyed bebe all the more. Pushing Dyalo's shoulder rudely, and adjusting her shawl, she said, 'May your face be disfigured, oye, you, the ill-omened one! Nee, you have killed me, although I'm still alive. I'm still breathing… Once Melu has immersed my ashes at Haridwar, you may wail and scream as much as you want to…'

And talking in this manner, when she made for the door, Dyalo became restless and stood up. She ran across, gripped her arm, and asked in a tearful voice, 'Now, where are you off to, bebe?'

'I'm going to jump into the well...or into the pond.' Speaking harshly, bebe pulled her arm free and then going towards the door, and mumbling to herself, said, 'Their children are crying out of hunger there, and here, she wants to know, where I'm going. One must know what time of the day it is, and not just call out, unnecessarily. Who knows when this old bull may begin to act wise! This bloody emaciated, old pest!' Still annoyed with Dyalo, she came out muttering, and proceeded to Finnah's house.

Dyalo was completely limp. Of course, her bebe was very much in the habit of babbling like this, and even walking out of the house at all odd hours. But she had never spoken in such a harsh and demeaning tone. Previously, whenever Dyalo had held her arm to drag her back into the house, she would simply say things like, 'Where could I go?' or 'Where will I go?' and then come back without any fuss, lie down on the manji, and start blabbering, but not go out again. Today, she had left as though she had no intention of ever coming back.

Her face covered with a chunni, Dyalo continued to stand in the doorway for some time. Then she shut the door, and came away. On reaching the door of the kothri, she suddenly thought of the she-calf. Dragging her feet, she went towards the cowshed. The she-calf was sitting, with its head down. The torn gunny sack, with which it had been covered, now lay under its rear feet. When she tried to pull the gunny sack from under it in a bid to cover it again, the animal made such a mournful sound that it almost pierced her ears. The moment

Dyalo thought of its injured leg, she felt disheartened again. For a long time, sitting next to her, she scratched it beneath its ears and over its two-inch-long horns. With its head now resting at Dyalo's feet, it was as though the she-calf felt somewhat calmer than before. With its soft breath blowing over her feet, Dyalo felt warmth surging up inside, but then again, for no particular reason, her eyes turned moist and she felt restless. Pulling her feet away from the she-calf's face, she got up and walked in.

The lantern was still burning. She looked at Shinda lying with his eyes shut. Going over to bebe's manji, as she slowly lay down, the legs of the manji made a strange, creaking sound.

Reclining on the manji, Shinda raised his head and asked, 'Nee bhaine! Where is bebe?'

Dyalo could not think of an answer. Shinda asked again, 'Has bapu also gone with Labhu, sister?'

Out of sheer nervousness, she started chastising Shinda, 'Why must you bother? Why can't you go back to sleep?' She turned her face away, and stuffing one end of her chunni into her mouth, sank her teeth into it.

With fear lurking in his eyes, Shinda kept staring at the roof for a long time. Then turning to the wall, he heaved a sigh and lay down. He closed his eyes. After a while, his eyes opened. Turning over and reliving Dyalo's first act of chastisement, he said, 'Nee, bhaine! Is the she-calf really in pain?' Seeing that Dyalo had not moved at all, he asked, again, 'Bhaine, shall I go and see how it is? Henh?'

When Dyalo didn't speak, he got up, staring in her direction, and then padding across the room, let himself out. Dyalo continued to lie still, ramrod straight, staring at the roof's wooden rafters.

After some time, Shinda came back, limping and winced as

he said, 'Hai nee bhaine! My leg is really aching very badly... and the she-calf is also bleating bitterly...'

Dyalo got up hurriedly, and then scowling at him, nearly screamed, 'Who asked you to go out, you fool? Come and lie down on the manji...be sensible.'

Shinda actually got scared. Holding his breath, he came and lay down on the manji, pulling the quilt right over his head.

Dyalo was as breathless as though she had come running from the wilderness. Turning her back on Shinda, first she went towards the lantern and lowered its wick; she made it so low that different shapes inside the kothri began to dissolve into each other. Then wrapping the chunni around herself somewhat tightly, she went out into the courtyard.

The sky was overcast with stars, all shining luminously. The light of the moon still shone, though it was surrounded on all sides by rolling, grey and white clouds. The clouds looked rather like the thick layers of mud-lime on the walls. Beneath the clouds, a long row of houses lay steeped in dense fog, as though it had penetrated every nook and cranny of the village. It appeared as though the families, living along a row of trees on the margins of the village, were now lost to the world. She was standing in the rear courtyard, facing Finnah's house from where she could hear some muffled voices, as dim as the dying flame of the lantern. The voice of Finnah's bebe rose above this hum, distinct and separate from all other voices.

Suddenly, there came the sound of two people squabbling from behind Finnah's house. Engaged in a heated argument, they were walking towards the dharamshala. Moving closer to the door, when she looked in that direction, she saw standing there, with a huge earthen bowl on his head, Kalu, telling the panch in his characteristic monotone, 'Then, how will we survive? How can we think of giving up this ritualistic practice we have been observing since the time of our forefathers?'

'If there is no eclipse for another two years, then what will you survive on?' The panch was trying to hold his ground and his voice was harsh, 'It's because you aren't willing to give up such ritualistic practices that you have been dragging on like this since the times of your forefathers.'

'But this is God's will; what right do we have to change it? And if this ritual exists, we will have to perform it…no?'

'To hell with these worldly rituals!' It was the first time Dyalo had heard such talk from the panch. 'When I'm telling you to be the son of a man and go back home…or do I give you your share of "alms in the name of a blind horse" here itself?'

Kalu was completely thrown off-balance. Looking furtively towards the lathi that the panch stood holding, barring his way, he spoke as he retreated, 'If you are so annoyed with me, bhai, then I'll go back. Why do you talk unnecessarily? Henh, bhai?'

Kalu went back home. The panch proceeded towards the dharamshala, and on seeing two persons standing there, started telling them in an unusually loud voice, 'Go, and announce it in the entire vehra that, today, no one is going into the village to ask for grain.'

Both the persons disappeared into the vehra, close on Kalu's heels. The panch walked away towards the village.

While stepping away from the door, Dyalo looked up at the moon shining overhead; one part of it, almost a fourth, had turned black. And as she stood watching, a pale cloud came swirling and swallowed up the moon. With this, the dense fog floating over the terraces of the village houses became all the more dark and inky. And an eerie silence lay all around.

That very moment, tearing into this silence like a piece of cloth being rent, a shrill scream was heard from the west end of the village.

'Alms in the name of the blind horse...bhai, oye...'

'Alms in the name of the blind horse...eh...eh.'

This was the voice of Giddhu, the one-eyed one, who lived in the fields of the sarpanch. His voice was as much of a bad omen as was his face. Seeing his misshapen body, dark-skinned face, torn clothes, and single eye, the children would often feel scared. It had been years since he had come into the vehra. From the sarpanch's house to his fields and back to his house—this was what the purpose of his entire life appeared to have become.

Dyalo felt as though Giddhu's voice sent tremors through her. A cold numbness rose from her feet, travelling up. But she didn't enter the kothri, feeling as though a dark fear had besieged her heart. The open door of the kothri appeared to her as gruesome as Giddhu's dark face, its jaw always hanging low; she feared that if she walked in, it would devour her alive. And the sky overhead appeared to be no less portentous. It looked somewhat like a mud wall, plastered with soggy dung-cakes, washed over by winter rains.

'Nee bhaine! Nee bhaine!' Shinda came limping from inside, trembling with fear. Throwing his arms around her waist, he said, 'There is a shadow of a witch, right behind our trunk.'

And then, screaming, he almost fell unconscious. Holding him in her arms, and bending over him, she shook him repeatedly, but he didn't move. With his arm around her shoulder, she brought him in and placed him on the manji. Raising the wick of the lantern, she first looked towards the trunk, and then at Shinda. Dark shadows were still etched on his face. Seated on the arm of the manji, she started staring at his face as though she, too, was on the verge of losing her consciousness, oblivious to what she could possibly do in this situation.

Suddenly, she felt as though dust motes were irritating her eyes. She let out a sigh, and even called out to him, 'Weh, veera!' in a bid to bring him back to his senses. Then, placing her head on his shrunken chest, she started sobbing.

After a while, Shinda suddenly woke up, as if from a deep slumber, and was now caressing her head with both his hands, like a wise old man, 'Bhaine, what's the matter? Why are you crying?... Henh? You crazy one!... Stop crying now. What are you crying for? Is everything fine?... Henh? I'll kill that witch!'

When Dyalo lifted her head from his chest and looked at Shinda's face, he was smiling. But his smile struck terror in her heart. Wiping her eyes, she asked, 'What happened, veer? Did you feel scared?'

'When?' Shinda got up and spoke in a confident voice, 'What kind of fear, bhaine?'

'All right, sleep now.'

'No, you go to sleep. I'll stay awake and wait till bebe and bapu return. All right?... Look, why don't you sleep here? I'll go and check on the she-calf...that crazy one may have thrown off the gunny sack once again.'

And talking in this wise manner, he went out to the courtyard.

Sitting there, Dyalo kept looking towards the door. She felt a sense of calm descend on her temporarily, but then, the same fears began to haunt her all over again. She came out hastily. Shinda was settling the gunny sack over the back of the she-calf. The sky still appeared to be the same—dark and inky. And the voice of Giddhu, the one-eyed one, was still screeching over the terraces, like a blunt sickle, and appeared to be whistling and screaming around the village, like a swirling dust storm.

'Alms in the name of the blind horse...bhai, oye...'

'Alms in the name of the blind horse...eh...eh...'